A Mythos of Monsters and Madness:

Horror Stories by Jeremiah Dylan Cook

This is a work of fiction.

Cover Art by **Rooster Republic**

Cover design by **Rooster Republic** & **Mariah Cook**

First Edition

ISBN 979-8-218-77034-1

Library of Congress Control Number: 2025918669

A New Pulp Tales Book

www.NewPulpTales.com

For Mariah, the first reader of these monstrous myths.

Contents

Reader Beware

This collection contains scenes of explicit

violence and gore.

Part 1

Graveyards Gone Wrong

Feeding Time

It will be here soon. The last rays of sun start to vanish behind the trees at the edge of the cemetery. I step out of the shadow to linger in the light. The heat difference between the two is stark in October. Mr. Johnson still kneels at his daughter's grave. He can't be here when the creature arrives, or I'll have an extra hole to dig tomorrow.

He looks up at me as I linger by the old oak, near the fence. His expression says it all. Why aren't you leaving me to grieve in peace? People look at me and see a gravedigger, but my true purpose is keeping them safe from what lurks in the woods.

Conversation isn't my strong suit, but I walk over to him. "Terribly sorry, but the cemetery is closing now."

Anger flashes across his features, but Mr. Johnson gets up. He dusts the fresh dirt and grass from his pants and walks off down the path to the exit. He's lucky he won't see what comes next. There's no stopping the beast. I can only satiate it for a little while, and fresh meat works the best. When I'm sure Mr. Johnson is out of sight, I sink my spade in the grave I finished filling in only three hours before.

The digging goes quickly because I know what's coming. There isn't time to lollygag. There isn't even time for a smoke break, though God knows I need one. I quit the habit at my wife's behest last March, but this is the one night a month I cheat. The sun's still up, but I am deep in the shade now. Autumn's cold winds cut through my thin jacket.

The situation used to be a lot worse than feeding it a corpse on occasion. Native Americans told tales about it penetrating their villages and absconding with whole families. They tried to warn the English settlers about the predator, but their warnings got misinterpreted as threats, and as often happened back then, it led to bloodshed. That only drew the thing closer to the settlers. After a few years of losing their kin, they took the Native Americans' advice and started giving it offerings to keep it from growing too ravenous.

My shovel reaches the coffin. I made sure not to bury the Johnson girl too deep. This is my thirteenth year of feeding the fiend, not my first rodeo. I even worked out a deal with the local mortuary so that they don't fully embalm the folks sent up here. My predecessor tried feeding the thing a poisoned corpse once, and that's why he's my predecessor. The sheriff never did find all the parts of him.

The smell of rot hits my nose as I reveal the deceased to the world again. The poor woman passed in a car accident a week ago. Nothing so heinous as dying young, except maybe the creature. I haul her out of the grave as gently as I can manage. Then I look away as I remove her clothing. This part always makes me sick, but when the thing left ruined pieces of fabric strewn about the forest, people asked too many questions. My body shakes from the increasing cold.

Just as I toss the clothes back into the pit, dirt I'd piled outside falls back in. It's the first indication that the beast's approaching. The last rays of sunlight are extinguished beyond the horizon, leaving the cemetery in darkness. I look up, but there's no sign of the moon or stars. Weatherman said a storm would be rolling in tonight. Looks like it's nearly here.

Trees crash in the distance, and I decide to fill the grave back in after the body's been taken. I look to the edge of the forest, where the trees tower over the tombstones, and hear more sounds of foliage being trampled. No more time to wait. I hightail it down the path to my truck. Once inside, I lock the doors and roll up the windows.

My breath fogs up the glass as I monitor the situation. The body is still visible, but I try not to let my eyes focus on it. She's dead, and I'm sure she'll suffer no pain, but the guilt of offering someone's physical remains up for food never goes away.

The thing steps out of the forest.

It's bone-white, standing nearly as tall as the old oak tree. I know it will change into a rust-like color after it feeds. My predecessor hypothesized that was due to the blood it absorbs while eating. The thing reaches out a skeletal hand toward the body but hesitates. Its yellow eyes roll up to lock on me.

My hand wanders over to the loaded gun on my passenger seat. I know it won't save me; hundreds have tried shooting it at one time or another. But if the thing decides it wants fresher meat, I won't go out meekly.

Our eyes remain locked, and I avoid letting my gaze drift down to its jagged teeth. Moments seem to stretch into hours. Every ounce of my survival instinct begs me to turn the truck on and floor it, but I resist. In the silence, I can hear ragged breathing outside. The thing's fingers tighten around the body, and it turns around.

When it disappears back into the forest, I let my panic manifest in great gulps of air. It's been years since it noticed my presence. The shooting pain in my arm worries me. It might be a heart attack.

The creature won't be content unless it's fed regularly, and I haven't trained a replacement yet.

The Hungry Cemetery

After an hour of hiking to the car and back for the bottles of water I'd forgotten, I returned to the small, moldering cemetery to find my friends missing. The graveyard we were restoring was confined by a square fence of deteriorating wrought iron. Within, the ground was hilly from years of decomposing corpses, which had created depressions in the earth. Tombstones jutted up at odd angles and leaned precariously. Several markers had fallen flat. Knee-high weeds ruled everything, except the center of the plot where a dead, crooked tree sprouted from the earth like a skeletal limb. The entire space wasn't much larger than a mausoleum.

There was clear evidence that my friends had started working. The broken pieces of the fence had been collected and put in a neat pile. Doug's manual lawnmower, the best option for attacking the uneven space, leaned against the bleak tree, next to a freshly mowed grave. Our rain jackets, including Stan's bright orange eyesore, remained where we'd left them outside the lone gap in the fence. Tired of carrying the waters, I set them down next to the jackets. With my hands finally free, I wiped the sweat from my forehead. I realized I'd torn the sleeve of my grey hooded sweatshirt on a passing branch, but my jeans had survived the trek unscathed. Overhead, dark clouds veiled the midday sun.

"Guys?" My voice echoed through the silent forest.

Unsure what else to do, I began circumventing the fence. Doug, Stan, and I had discovered this place a week ago because we'd been going stir crazy. None of us were experienced hikers, but an entrance to the Appalachian Trail lay five miles from our shared apartment in Carlisle, Pennsylvania. Stan had insisted that we get out to see nature. He'd spent some of his youth in the boy scouts, and he always poked fun at Doug and me for being too reliant on the comforts of city living. Thunder echoed in the distance, and I turned to look back down the trail.

The path weaved out of the forest across harvested farmland and into a separate patch of trees. The week before, we'd all been amazed at what we found as we ventured further from our car, which we'd left parked in a dirt lot at the trailhead. We'd crossed two little bridges, spanning creeks that gushed with water from recent storms, spotted several deer, and chatted with a group of athletic sorority girls who'd also decided to spend their day exploring nature. When we discovered this decrepit cemetery, Doug proposed cleaning it to meet our school's service obligation. Our university required us to spend eight hours a semester helping our community. Doug surmised that the plot had been previously owned by an unknown local family named Chambers, due to the surname's prevalence on all the least faded stones, some of which dated back to the 1700s. Unfortunately, after we returned to civilization that day, none of us had been able to locate any further information on the property. It was like it had been erased from public record.

I completed my walk around the rusted barrier, but my friends remained missing. They couldn't have returned to the car without passing me on the trail. Neither of them liked playing practical jokes, and they'd both been jazzed about putting in the time to clean this place up, so I didn't think they were trying to shirk out of our shared responsibility. Another crash of thunder startled me, and lightning flashed over the farmland beyond the trees.

My friends might've gone further down the path, searching for shelter from the approaching storm. Doug, always the smart one in our trio, would've spotted the incoming downpour on the horizon. I assumed they'd left their jackets here to inform me that they were still nearby. I stepped onto the trail and heard a gasp for air behind me. I spun back toward the cemetery.

Stan's blonde-haired head jutted out of the freshly mowed grave near the crooked tree in the center of the burial ground.

The scene was so surreal that I froze in place. I tried to puzzle out what had occurred. I pictured my friends falling into a cavity created by the rotting bodies beneath the soil.

"Joel, help," Stan wormed his hands out of the dirt on each side of him.

Snapped out of my paralyzing analysis, I ran toward my friend. Stan was only a few feet away. I jumped over the fence. When I landed on the hilly earth, a subtle quake reminded me of how cranberry sauce wobbles when dumped from a can. My shins were submerged in a sea of overgrown vegetation. I went to take a step forward when the ground in front of me snapped open.

A gaping maw stared up at me with the cemetery's collected skeleton's contributing their rotting limbs as improvised teeth. A crimson glow shined from the pit's depths, and warm, rancid air issued forth. The mouth of dirt gnashed the bones together repeatedly, trying to seize my foot, which hovered above the hole. I pushed myself away, and a twisted piece of fence scraped my shoulder.

Stan gestured for me to back up. "It's not going to let you get close to me."

Adrenaline pumped into my veins as the earth beneath me trembled again. I hopped back over the fence. Outside the cemetery, the ground was solid and normal. Inside, it continued to writhe like a living thing. Sweat poured off me as my heart jackhammered in my chest. Reality itself had fundamentally changed before my eyes. If I'd been into drugs, I could've told myself that I'd only witnessed a horrific hallucination, but I'd avoided anything harder than whiskey to this point in life. Stan screamed, and the imminent danger to my friend forced me back into the moment.

Unwilling to reenter the cemetery, I frantically searched for something that I could use to reach Stan. I identified a long branch that would work, picked it up, and ran to the gap in the fence. While I remained at the edge of the wrought iron partition, I offered the end of the wood to my friend.

Stan had managed to free most of his upper body while I'd been hunting for the means to help him escape further. His white t-shirt was stained brown from his time submerged in dirt. Stan grabbed onto the branch, and I pulled. My friend didn't seem to move at all.

"It's getting tighter," Stan screamed.

I pulled harder, and the branch snapped in two. The force of my exertion sent me falling to the ground. Pain surged from where I'd cut my shoulder on the fence, but I scrambled back up.

The earth around Stan fell away and released him. He tried to climb out of the hole. His waist reappeared, covered in grime, then his legs. Just as he was about to get his ankles out, the earth snapped shut.

His feet were gone in a blink, and blood oozed out of his jeans from his remaining ankle stumps. Stan collapsed onto the dirt between two tombstones. I expected him to scream, but he stayed focused on escaping as he crawled toward the gap in the fence, where I waited. He was barely visible as he snaked his way through the grasping weeds.

I leaned in as far as I could without stepping into the hungry graveyard. As I reached for Stan's hand, I caught sight of the name on the nearest tombstone. It appeared to be freshly carved, and today's date was chiseled in. I recognized my missing friend's first name, Doug, combined with the family's last name, Chambers. The twisted tree in the cemetery's center loomed overhead, and a menacing smile formed in the ancient bark. Stan's clammy fingers touched mine. The ground beneath my friend opened again as I grasped his hand.

I yanked him forward, but at the same time, he slid into the opening hole.

To my relief, I managed to pull him out, and we tumbled backward. He landed on me. We weren't out of the woods yet, but I'd gotten Stan free of the cemetery. I went to gently move Stan from atop me, and I realized with sickening clarity that he didn't weigh enough.

Something warm flowed over me. Looking down, I confirmed my fear. Stan's body was missing below his abdomen. Blood soaked into my clothes as his intestines sloughed out of his body between my legs. I stared into Stan's lifeless blue eyes as the sound of scraping stone drew my attention to where we'd just escaped.

A new tombstone erupted from the earth with the name Stan Chambers.

Lost Vintage

When I came to at the hospital, the authorities informed me I'd been found near death by fellow hikers. My rescuers assumed I'd been mauled by a bear, but they couldn't explain why I'd been discovered amongst the ruins of a broken window. For that scene in the middle of the woods, they had no explanation. One cop I spoke with asked if I'd been hiking in the wilderness carrying a huge pane of glass, and I decided to go along with that ridiculous notion because I thought it would make more sense to the police than my memories.

Hours Earlier

Emerging from the trees, I pushed my hair from my face and retied my ponytail. Ahead, the Appalachian Trail cut through a large swath of harvested farmland before re-entering the forest. A small, gated and overgrown cemetery lay just inside the woods there.

I'd worn comfortable jeans and my favorite sweatshirt for the hike, thinking it would be a cool day. Instead, I was overheated. I removed my water bottle from my backpack and took a long swallow. The sip began to replenish the sweat dripping off my forehead, but thunder startled me into spilling my follow-up gulp. Dark clouds approached from the horizon, blotting out the October sun. I could've called an early quit to the hike, but it would've been an hour before I got back to my car. Tornados weren't usual in Central Pennsylvania, but the oddly hot day colliding with the typical fall chill made one seem possible. The flash of a movement drew my gaze from the impending downpour back to the cemetery.

A woman in a flowing, crimson dress beckoned me nearer.

Intrigued, I returned my bottle to my bag and approached. I examined the lonely resting spot in better detail as I grew nearer. The fence was wrought iron, but it had been covered in rust, and pieces were missing in several places. Inside, headstones so old the names were worn off sprouted from the dirt alongside three crooked trees which had grown into a tangle of branches covering the unkept grass. Another crack of thunder caused me to increase my pace toward the graveyard as shadowy tendrils from the storm's edge reached in my direction. I made it under the orange, red, and yellow leaves as a deluge erupted from the clouds.

"I can show you to better shelter." The woman said.

"I'll probably just wait it out. Storms this powerful don't usually last long." I turned to get a better sense of the stranger. Her winged eyeliner was expertly applied, and her curly, black hair was streaked with neon blue highlights. "Are you out here to film a vlog or something?"

The woman smiled. "Why do you ask that?"

"Well, you look great, and this trail doesn't usually get many knockouts strolling along dressed to impress. Although, I've never actually made it this far down the path before."

"You don't look bad yourself."

"That'd be all the hiking." I flirted back, hoping I wasn't misreading her intentions. It'd been almost a year since Beth left, and I needed a confidence boost. "My name's Sonia, by the way. I'll be your companion while mother nature lets off some steam."

Lightning flashed overhead, and the rain fell from the leaves in titanic plops.

"Well, the earth certainly deserves a chance to vent its rage. I'm Camilla."

A frigid chill cut the warm day to pieces.

"Pleased to make your acquaintance." I set my backpack down and used it as a seat.

Camilla pulled a cigarette from inside her low-cut neckline. "You got a light?"

"Sorry. I don't smoke."

"Pity. A good smoke is hard to come by these days."

The wind sent Camilla's dress whipping back and forth, and I glanced down to see the woman's feet were encased in grave soil.

I gestured to the ground. "What's going on there?"

All warmth melted out of Camilla's face. "The house is right there. I recommend you visit. This storm's only going to get worse."

I turned to look where Camilla indicated and saw a large Victorian mansion nestled in the trees, just off the trail. The home had an enormous wraparound porch with ornately carved wooden arches running underneath the roof. Paint peeled off the structure, but I could still make out the bright blue hue from its heyday. A large, circular window was set in the lone steeple on the third floor, where a shadowy figure loomed. I assumed it was a trick of the cloud darkened day, but the sight made my skin crawl. I turned to ask Camilla about the house, and she was gone.

My heart pounded faster. I hopped off my backpack and surveyed the area for any sign of Camilla's red dress. The feeling that I was being watched grew eerily stronger as I searched the forest surrounding the cemetery for any sign of my lost companion.

"Camilla?" I approached the spot she'd been.

An unlit cigarette in the dirt was all that remained. I bent down to grab the item and confirm its tactile existence. As my fingers touched the paper, the earth swallowed me.

I landed hard on rocky ground a few feet below. Above, rain misted into the pit through the tree cover. A worm wiggled across my nose, and I screamed in revulsion, shaking my head to get it off.

Adrenaline kept the pain at bay as I got to my feet. Nothing seemed broken. I reached up to attempt to climb back out, but I couldn't make the ascent. The opening was a leg's length from my fingertips.

"Can anybody hear me? Help!"

There came no answer, except for the continuing storm. I pulled out my phone, but I couldn't get a signal in the hole. The screen's light illuminated a smooth, rectangular stone in front of me. I stepped forward and found empty sconces lining a staircase leading upward.

Unsure about venturing further into the unknown, I sat down on the first step. My pack was lying by the cemetery. Someone would notice it eventually. All I had to do was wait.

Lightning blazed across the sky above and struck the tree providing the most shelter to my pit. Wood creaked as a charred branch splintered from its flaming trunk. Water poured into the hole from the gap created by the destroyed foliage above. I backed up a step as a pool formed on the rocky ground. Washed in by the storm, a severed tree branch nearly speared me as it struck the dirt wall beside my shoulder. The soil crumbled apart to reveal a deteriorating wooden coffin.

The sound of scratching came from inside.

I imagined a rat gnawing through the wood to get at me. Instead of waiting within the flooding cemetery, I decided to try my luck with the unknown passage. Turning around, I started climbing the steps.

The air grew warmer as I ascended. My phone light kept the darkness at bay, but my battery was draining quickly. I'd be forced to shut it off soon if I wanted to save it for any future calls.

The sound of splintering wood echoed up from the depths, and I paused.

Listening carefully, I heard something scrape over the steps behind me. After another moment, there was a second scrape, followed by a third. I turned and held my phone light toward the darkness. The glow didn't make it all the way down the steps.

My breathing blared in my ears as I waited for something to step into the light. "Somebody there?"

Time slowed to a crawl. The glare of my phone dimmed, and I hit the screen in a panic to bring it back to full power. The darkness on the steps below remained unchanged. Nothing answered my inquiry. Silence reigned.

Unsure whether I was relieved or disappointed, I turned back up the stairs. Something ahead of me glimmered in my phone's light. I approached cautiously.

Rows of bottles were stored on a crumbling wooden wine rack. Webs and dust covered all, but I pulled one of the bottles out to inspect it. Wiping away the grime revealed an unknown label, *W. Chambers, 1895*. The liquid inside was practically black, but I could just detect the slightest hue of scarlet. I returned the bottle and checked another, *A. Bierce, 1886*. The scraping sound echoed up from the depths again. This time the noise repeated rapidly and grew louder on every occurrence.

Panic seized me, and I gripped the bottle tightly as I turned to face the approaching presence. I lifted my light to uncover whatever hid in the staircase, but I again saw nothing as the sound ceased. "You have one more chance to announce yourself if you're following me."

A surge of frustration forced me to toss the bottle down the stairway. It was swallowed by darkness, but I didn't hear the glass smash. Instead, there was a single thump followed by the sound of the liquid sloshing about inside its container. Something had stopped the bottle's destruction.

I backed away from the staircase and crossed over a threshold into a new room. An old, open door connected this space with the wine cellar and graveyard tunnel. I surveyed the area hastily, trying to keep my focus on the darkened steps. I'd found my way into a basement filled with tarped furniture. Dull gray light peeked in from four window slits atop opposite walls. A single staircase led further up. With any luck, I'd be back on the trail outside in minutes. The scraping sound resumed, and I returned my focus to the steps I'd just left.

A white, spindly form emerged from the darkness at the edge of the steps, near the wine rack. In its skeletal hand hung the bottle I'd thrown. My heart threatened me with cardiac arrest as I slammed the door shut. To my relief, a lock on the door latched into place. I considered moving one of the tarped objects in front of the door for extra reinforcement but decided to head straight for the steps. The faster I could get back outside, the better.

I tested the moldering wood before trusting it with my weight, but I was pleasantly surprised by the sturdiness as I ascended. On the top step, I heard knocking from the door I'd shut below. My pulse raced, and I continued up to the first floor, ignoring the increasing urgency of the knocks.

A rotting kitchen greeted me outside the basement. Rusted pans sat in the sink, and vines grew over the decrepit cabinets. The windows were boarded up, but light still slithered in from the cracks to make my phone's illumination unnecessary. I still had no signal, and I turned it off to save the battery.

"You came." Camilla stood, smiling in front of the sink. "Abraham will be so happy to have a guest."

Frozen by the unexpected reappearance of the woman, I felt my hands shaking.

"He'll want to see you. He's upstairs. Hasn't left this house since he read that dammed play." Camilla gestured to the next room.

I blinked, and she was gone again. The knocking downstairs intensified. Wind howled through the house from the storm as branches scraped against the siding.

There was no way I'd stay any longer than necessary. I certainly didn't plan to go upstairs. Instead of following Camilla's direction, I went the opposite way and entered a boarded-up room with a torn-up chaise lounge, several splintered chairs, and a water damaged grand piano in the corner. Glass crunched under my sneakers as I walked across the room. Fragments of a formerly ornate light fixture were scattered on the floor. With no way out in sight, I moved to the next room.

Here, my heart's hammering started to slow as the back door stared me in the face. I hurried over to it and grabbed the handle. It didn't move at first, but I managed to turn it with a little extra effort. I heard the mechanism working inside the door. I pulled hard. Nothing happened. I pushed instead. Nothing happened. Frustrated, I threw my weight into the door. It rattled but didn't budge. Sweat started to accumulate on my brow as I continued to try to force it open.

At last, I quit and headed back into the room I'd come from. The piano began to play, slowly, out of tune. Even in its horrid form, I recognized Beethoven's Moonlight Sonata.

Staring at the piano, with no player and the lid closed, I started laughing at the sheer insanity of the situation. As if drawn by my mirth, phantom forms appeared around me, dancing to the music. I counted eight individuals, four men and three women, wearing the finery of the Victorian era. The men dressed in vests and long-tailed coats. The women wore corsets and bustles with ruffles and lace draping. The scent of smoke filled the air, and I coughed.

"Guess I should've dressed up," I said.

"Nonsense." Camilla stepped from the other room with an empty wine bottle. "You're perfect as you are."

She offered me the bottle. The label read: *Sonia, 2020.*

I took the bottle and smashed it in her face.

Instead of a shocked reaction, cries of pain, or blood, Camilla vanished along with the apparitions and discordant music.

Outside, the storm picked up again. I tightened my grip on the bottle bearing my name and marched back into the kitchen. From the basement, the knocks continued. Moving through the area, I turned a corner and faced the main staircase, which stood opposite a large front door that someone had covered with dozens of boards. It would take hours to pry the nails out, remove the wood, and escape that way. The same went for the boards covering all the windows I'd seen on the first floor. I took a breath and turned to ascend. I'd need to play Camilla's game.

Photos lined the steps. While dust obscured most of the details, I could make out two pictures as I climbed toward the second story. One was of the room with the piano, filled with guests. A lone figure stood in a robe holding a collection of papers up to the audience. The other was a framed ink drawing of two suns.

On the landing, I found the windows secured like they'd been on the lower level. The rug running through the hallway had been eaten by time, but I spotted a pristine white mask sitting atop an unblemished black pedestal at the end of the corridor. The air was stale, and I stepped cautiously as the wood under my feet creaked with every step. A small bronze plaque under the mask read: Performance Regalia. I considered picking up the object, but it felt so greasy to the touch that I recoiled as though I'd just touched the antenna of a centipede.

A door squeaked open behind me, and I spun, bottle raised high. Another set of stairs led to the attic. I shuddered at the memory of the shadowy figure I'd glimpsed up there when I'd been in the graveyard. If I'd thought I had any other way out, I wouldn't have gone up those stairs. Each step forward, the light seemed to dim further, despite the sizeable circular window coming into view. When I reached the top, the door at the bottom slammed shut.

My heart couldn't seem to beat any faster, and I felt my back starting to throb from my earlier fall. I'd exhausted the adrenaline that had kept me going without issue to this point. The room was small, but there was a large wingback chair in the right corner, with a small desk beside it. Atop the surface, a tumbler glass had been left out along with a bottle of dark, crimson liquid. The label read, *Camilla, 2015.*

Outside the large window, the trail I'd walked to get to the cemetery was visible. Lightning flashed, and thunder shook the house, but blue sky and sunlight appeared on the horizon. The storm was nearly over.

"Fill the bottle." Camilla now sat in the chair, holding a dull, dinner knife toward me. "Give us your blood to store in the wine cellar, and we'll let you leave."

I took the knife, but I slipped it into my pocket. "No deal."

"I'll have to let him convince you." Camilla pointed behind me.

As I turned around, the smell of rotting meat assaulted my nostrils. A man in a hooded robe stepped from the darkened corner of the attic opposite Camilla. His face was obscured, but I could see that while time had turned his outfit black, it had initially been a shade of yellow.

"Let me introduce Abraham Van Strauss," Camilla said. "He was once a wealthy railroad baron. At the height of his power, Abe threw bohemian parties for his decadent friends. When he heard about a play that had been banned for indecency, Abe just had to read it to them. As they gathered, he surprised his guests by adding in another twist. The person Abe had bought the play from told him all about how to arrange a little ritual to go along with the play's performance. The results were supposed to bring longer life to everyone involved. This was during the height of the Spiritualism craze, so you can imagine the guests were eager to believe things like this worked. Surprisingly, those who attended the party found themselves without flesh by the end of the night, and old Abe was trapped in his home forever."

"Were you one of his guests?" I asked.

Camilla idly fingered the tumbler sitting next to her. "God, no. I found his mansion while I was legend tripping with some friends. The house moves around, so it's quite a challenge to locate. My pals didn't give up their blood when asked, but I did."

"Spill your—" Abraham coughed mid-sentence. "Blood." He spat an inky wad of phlegm onto the floor. "Or we'll be forced to spill it for you."

The last vestiges of the storm pummeled the home, but I could see sunlight growing nearer.

"Why do you need it?" I asked.

"We don't answer to you," Camilla said. "Do you think I was so insolent as to ask that question?"

"I'm sure you wished you had," I said.

Camilla looked at the bottle next to her and smiled. "Yes. I wish I had, but it's too late for me."

"But not for me." I moved away from Abraham and Camilla to stand with my back to the window. I held the bottle out to ward off any attacks, and I withdrew the knife from my pocket. "You can't keep me here. Someone will come looking, and I'm not giving up my blood. What's the alternative?"

Abraham threw his hood back to reveal an exceedingly elderly visage. The skin sagged off his face and only the slightest wisps of snowy hair remained atop his head. His eyes were sunken pits with sickly, yellowed pupils. "We could've done this the easy way."

The door at the bottom of the attic steps opened, and I saw the white form from the cemetery tunnel take the first step up.

My jaw dropped, and I felt tremors seize my body.

It would've been too simple to call it a skeleton. The figure was undoubtedly comprised of bones, but I spotted several skulls, multiple arms, and various legs sticking out from its exposed rib cage at different angles. Every piece of it seemed to move with its own mind, as fingers twitched aimlessly, and jaws snapped open and closed at different speeds. Despite its impractical shape, it moved swiftly toward me.

In a panic, I threw the bottle into the ascending collection of skeletal parts. This time it didn't catch the object, and the bottle shattered against the figure. The force was enough to momentarily halt it, but I knew it wouldn't be permanently stopped. I spun around and prepared for my only escape. Abraham shambled forward to stop me, but I slashed at him with the knife. To my surprise, his entire hand came off from the strike. Dust poured out of his open wound. With a moment's respite, I flung myself at the attic window.

It shattered, and I plummeted to the earth, screaming. Glass shards littered the ground from my exit, but the soil was soft and muddy due to the rain. Blood soaked into my clothes and tinted everything scarlet.

Camilla appeared next to me. "Well done. I wasn't as brave as you."

Over her shoulder, the entire Victorian mansion started to shimmer and then vanished. She followed. The storm clouds rolled away, and I was left broken and in pain.

Part 2

Horrid Hazel Peak

Legend Trip

The decaying Victorian mansion loomed over the three of us as the sun set behind its lone steeple.

"Camilla, get in the shot." Josh adjusted his camera's tripod. "Before we lose the light."

I stepped into the shadow of the building, and a chill crept up my spine.

Dave stared at his script. "Remember your lines?"

"Yes, I'm good whenever you guys want to roll." I swung my head to drape my neon blue highlights into view.

"Action," Josh said.

"Tonight, I'll be investigating the Abraham Van Strauss Mansion. Originally built in Hazel Peak, Pennsylvania, in the 1800s, the structure currently sits on a forested hill five miles outside Broadalbin, New York. Confused? You should be. There are no records of anyone moving the mansion, but pictures of it have been uploaded online in places as far away as Bird City, Kansas. Thanks to one of my online supporters, I received a tip about its current location. So, how did it get here? Well, I intend to find out on another episode of Legend Trip."

"Cut." Dave tucked the script into his back pocket. "How'd the shot look?"

Josh gave a thumbs-up as he grabbed his camera-mounted tripod and picked his bag of equipment off the ground. "Let's get inside so I can set up the light for the interior shot."

The two of them stepped onto the porch that wrapped around the first floor. Ornately carved wooden arches ran underneath the second-story roof. Paint peeled from everywhere, and no signs of life were evident. A large, circular window peered out from the third-story spire, and the fading light cast inky shadows within. Josh pushed the front door open and disappeared into the mansion's darkness. A rotten smell wafted out of the breached interior.

"Maybe we should skip the inside?" I suggested.

Dave turned to glare at me. "Are you kidding me? After the three-hour drive and the hike through the woods? Hell no. We're paying you to be the eye candy for our web series, but if you'd rather bail on the money and find your own way home, be my guest."

"You can be a real fascist sometimes." I smoothed out my crimson dress, gave Dave a military salute, and made a show of marching into the mansion.

"Up here. This will be great for the background." Josh was already setting up on the second floor.

My eyes adjusted to the dim surroundings. Someone had boarded over all the windows from the inside, but tiny beams of light crept through the cracks. To the right, rusted pans lingered in the rotting kitchen, where vines grew over decrepit cabinets. Ahead, a large staircase led to where Josh was working. I walked up the creaking stairs with Dave at my heels.

Josh had arranged his camera and a small stage light opposite a black pedestal exhibiting a white mask. "Look, it's perfect for the next shot."

The second floor was a confining hallway with more boarded-up windows opposite a rickety banister. A closed door at the end of the corridor stood across from the object Josh had spotlighted. I moved closer. The piece reminded me of a Greek theater mask, except it had large holes for a person's eyes and none for their mouth. A plaque atop the pedestal read: Performance Regalia.

Dave appeared next to me, nodding his head negatively. "No way this is from the night the mansion vanished. Someone's messing with us. This thing looks a hundred years newer than anything else here. Josh is right though, it's great for the next shot. Why don't you put it on for the opening and take it off before speaking?"

As Dave rejoined Josh behind the camera, I reached out for the mask.

When I touched it, my hand was repulsed by its greasy texture. "No, thanks. It's dirty."

"It looks pristine," Dave argued.

"Can we just do the shot?" I spun to face them.

Josh hit a button on his camera. "I'm ready."

"Action." Dave said.

"As the name indicates, the man responsible for this mansion's construction was Abraham Van Strauss. He was a railroad tycoon who made his money shipping coal out of Northeastern Pennsylvania. When he wasn't working, he'd throw extravagant parties for his robber baron pals. During the height of the Spiritualism Movement, Strauss came into possession of a play that supposedly held supernatural qualities. No one knows the name of the play or anything about the content, but the night of the party where he intended to debut it, the mansion vanished from Hazel Peak along with all his guests. Only a hole remained where the structure had once stood. The newspapers were quick to declare that the abode had fallen into an abandoned mine shaft, but after I did some digging, I confirmed no mine ever ran under the Strauss Mansion. So, what happened that night?"

The door behind me slammed open, and we all jumped.

Dave let out a frustrated sigh. "Tell me that didn't ruin the take?"

Josh set to work re-watching the footage.

"You're not worried about that?" I looked at the open door, which revealed a staircase to the attic.

Dave walked over and looked up the stairs. "The wind."

"I can save it in editing." Josh gave us a thumbs up.

Behind Josh, a hooded man stood shrouded in darkness, blocking the stairs to the first floor. "Visitors are always welcome here, but you must provide an offering for your trespass."

Three wine bottles rolled from the darkness toward us. One stopped at Josh's feet as he spun around, and two made it to

Dave and me. I could see a name on the nearest bottle's label, Camilla.

The figure shambled forward and held out a dull, ancient knife. "Fill the bottle."

Josh laughed. "Hell, no."

The floor gave way beneath him, but he managed to lean forward and stop his upper body from being swallowed by the mansion. In his struggle to ascend, he knocked the light over. Before I could help, six skeletal hands reached up from the darkness and pulled him into the blackness below.

"He'll be set dressing for the play now. You two still have a choice." The overturned light revealed an ancient, wrinkled face beneath the figure's hood.

"It's Abraham Van Strauss," Dave shouted as he clambered over the second story banister in a panic.

"I'll take that as a no." Strauss flicked his wrist.

The banister crumbled to pieces, and Dave fell from the second floor. I didn't see where he landed, but I heard a sickening crunch. The floor in front of me reformed, and Strauss approached. I could see that while his robes had darkened with age, they'd initially been some shade of yellow.

I picked up the bottle bearing my name and accepted the knife.

Adrenaline numbed the pain as I cut into my forearm. It wasn't long before I marveled at how well the bloody contents matched my dress. My surroundings seemed to spin, and I felt like

I could sleep for days. Strauss collected my vintage and vanished. I stumbled back outside to find the surrounding forest replaced with a cornfield. The mansion had moved again. When I stepped off the front porch, I collapsed.

I didn't remember standing back up, but when I looked down, I saw my lifeless body remained where it had fallen.

The House Flipping Find

My story began a week ago when I found the thing that's doomed me. You see, I do a lot of work for this couple who flip homes in the area. My region of Northeastern Pennsylvania has tons of cheap houses that they can buy low and sell a little higher for profit. New Yorkers looking to get out of the city are the biggest suckers for the authentic mountain views. Anyway, one day I'm tearing out some cheap tile in a basement when I uncover the edge of an old wooden box. The thing looked ready to fall apart, and a little piece of me thought there might be some kind of treasure in it. I'd never forgotten the time a guy I'd worked with found a perfectly preserved copy of Action Comics Number One, where Superman first showed up. My old coworker ended up retiring on that. So, I hid the box from everyone else at the worksite. I know it seems a little greedy, but would you want to split a million bucks if you didn't have to?

Got the box to my apartment that night. Someone had put an old lock on it, but the thing was so rusted I managed to knock it off with one good hit from my hammer. My anticipation of treasure only grew, but when I lifted the worn-out hinges, I only found a plain leather book wrapped in cloth. Paging through it slowly, I realized it was a personal journal. I couldn't think of how to make any cash off it unless someone famous wrote it. The first page squashed my hopes. It listed the owner's name as Ursula Schmidt. I did a quick web search but couldn't find anyone of note. Disinterested in the journal at this point, I figured I'd donate it to the local library. They always need books from what I hear.

That night something odd happened. I didn't even consider the book and the event might be linked until I started writing this, but I'm sure they were. As I tried to sleep, I heard scratching on my roof. I figured it must be squirrels or birds, but the noise woke me from a sound sleep around midnight. I managed to get back to sleep pretty easily because the noise didn't last long.

I was off work the next day, and by noon I'd already tired of Xbox and couldn't decide on a show to watch amongst my four streaming apps. The journal lay on my coffee table, so I turned off the tv and lay back with it. I couldn't remember the last time I read anything. Maybe it hadn't been since high school? Anyway, here's what it said.

August 5th, 1792

Papa and Mama are both gone now. The doctor told me that the bullet Papa took in the war of independence must have finally reached his heart. They never could get it out. Mama got sick right after he passed. She started coughing up blood one evening and was cold as ice the next. The doctor suggested I move out of our house in the woods and into town. He even suggested I live in the small room next to his office. Every person in ten miles knows that is where he has his mistresses live. Why his wife puts up with it, I do not know. Perhaps I will feel different in the winter, but for now, I cannot imagine parting with the place I have lived my whole life. Papa built this house right after he arrived from Deutschland. My inheritance allows me to live freely, for now.

August 10th, 1792

I awoke to a frightful rapping on my door tonight. When I answered it, I met John Parsons on my front porch. He looked like the devil lapped at his heels, but I could see no one outside beside him.

"Ursula, you have to let me in," he said.

"I am a Christian woman, and I do not allow men who are not of my blood to stay the evening with me," I replied, just as Papa would have expected.

"It's going to get me if you don't let me in," he replied.

Had his demeanor not been so frantic, I probably would have told him to move along. But he genuinely seemed scared of whatever he had encountered in the woods. I thought that a wolf might be prowling around. Papa shot one nearby only a few days before he passed.

"Is it wolves?" I asked.

Parsons nodded like a mad man and began forward without waiting for my consent, but I did step aside to let him in.

I allowed him to get comfortable in my front room, while I locked myself in the bedroom. That is where I am writing by candlelight. I wonder what my parents would make of this if they were here. I know they would not judge my decision harshly, but

I hope the townsfolk will not begin to whisper that I am impure behind my back.

I think I hear that wolf prowling around outside. It must have been huge to scare Mr. Parsons. Well, thankfully, we are safe in the house for tonight. Now I must get some rest to handle whatever tomorrow brings.

August 11th, 1792

Lord, help me.

I awoke due to a cool breeze from my window this morning, but I did not remember opening it last night. My fear of the wolf would not allow such a thing, despite the sweltering heat of the last summer days. I found the door from my bedroom wide open as well. Had Mr. Parsons played me for a fool? If so, I thought I had been awfully lucky to have been unmolested by the man in the night.

When I walked into my front room, I found a scene like nothing I have yet witnessed in my sixteen years of life. Mr. Parsons lay on the floor, where he had intended to sleep, but his body was wrong. All wrong. He had been a young man of twenty-two when I left him last night. Now he looked older than anyone I ever saw. His skin was shriveled up and grayed. There did not seem to be a hint of blood left in him. I might have assumed he died of some strange disease if it was not for the single, large hole in his neck. It reminded me of Papa's old bullet wound.

I am gathering my things and heading into town. I need help to understand what happened here last night.

August 11th, 1792

So much has happened today.

The walk to town took a half-hour, and I kept glancing about for any sign of the wolf that might have pursued Mr. Parson's last night. I brought my papa's musket with me, but I have never been adept at shooting it. Unless I could have killed the beast in one shot, it would have gotten me for sure when I needed to reload it. Even Papa couldn't get the powder and lead ball lodged into the barrel very fast.

Thankfully, I made it to Hazel Peak without incident. In Europe, my papa told me they have towns that span as far as the eye can see, but this one only goes four buildings in every direction. Most people live farther out in the woods on farmland, like my papa and mama. It seemed to me that folks in the town gave me suspicious looks as I made my way to John Barnabas's home. He heads the local militia, and my papa served with him in the war. On his deathbed, Papa told me to go to him if I needed any help after he was gone.

Mr. Barnabas welcomed me into his home politely, and I provided him with my tale from the previous evening. His face seemed to drain of blood as I described Mr. Parson's neck wound. Then he began backing away from me.

"You need to leave now," he said.

"But what shall I do about the body in my home?" I asked.

"Whatever you like. I don't think it matters much."

He would not answer any further questions from me, and when I tried to approach him, he backed away quickly. I went straight across town to Pastor Edgar. His reaction to my story was similar to Mr. Barnabas's, but he didn't shoo me right out the door. Instead, he told me a story that chilled me to the core.

Pastor Edgar stood at the front of his church, behind the small wooden alter my family donated. "You should not have let Mr. Parsons over your threshold. You will be damned for it, unless—"

"Unless what?" I asked.

"Did Mr. Parsons touch you when he entered your residence?"

I struggled to recall for a long moment. "He may have."

The priest's gaze left me to stare at the floor. "I do not know where it comes from, but I can only assume the beast is in league with the devil. It only comes at night, and it's been seen in these woods since before Hazel Peak was founded. Some say it's a curse left by the Lenape, but natives passing through the area were the first ones to warn me about the creature. What they called it sounded like "Hmukwam," and the translator told me the name roughly corresponded to "blood creature." Once you have touched a person it marked, you will be hunted until—"

"Tell me, I can handle the truth," I said, not sure if I could.

"Until your end is the same as Mr. Parsons."

After that, he implored me to take a cross, for whatever protection it could provide, and leave, to avoid spreading the curse to others. Walking home, I struggled to recall if Mr. Parson's had truly touched me. My memory was incredibly hazy on the subject. It was just as possible that he grazed my shoulder as he did not.

I barricaded my homestead as best as possible when I returned. The windows are shuttered, and the heat is now stifling. I moved my bed into the pantry, where it would stop the door from opening. This is the safest I think I can make myself.

Unfortunately, it is sweltering in here. The candlelight adds to the already disgusting temperature. I must soon cease writing. I hope that in the morning I will feel foolish for taking this precaution. Maybe there will be no noises or horrors at all.

August 12th, 1792

This morning has brought me joy. Nothing woke me once I had drifted off to sleep in the pantry. When I emerged this morning, nothing in the house looked amiss. I had a great laugh about the entire ordeal.

August 12th, 1792

My relief proved to be momentary. When I ventured outside to gather wood, I came across great scratches upon the sides of the house. They were three in number, and the depth of the strikes spoke to a startling length of the creature's claws. I also discovered many more scratches around the windows, but the shutters had held against assault. I must have been too insulated in the pantry to hear the noises.

August 12th, 1792

I spent most of the day trying to decide if I should sneak back into town. Maybe whatever has my scent would not come for me in the midst of so many people? But I also fear to do harm to my neighbors. They are too cowardly to help me, but I am unsure if I would do any different if our roles were reversed. In the end, I decided to spend another night barricaded inside the pantry. Perhaps it will grow tired of trying to get at me and move on?

August 13th, 1792

This morning brought more destruction to my home. Papa would weep to see it in such a condition. Whatever hunts me broke one of the shutters open. Once it got inside, it seemed to knock into every piece of furniture we owned. I awoke to the sound of Mama's cherished dishes crashing to the ground. It was not long until a scratching came to the pantry door. The thought of what I might have seen trying to get under the bottom of the door, if I had been brave enough to light a candle, brings me to tears. What will I do?

August 13th, 1792

I nearly lost myself in desolation this morning, but I have risen above my base fears and grief this afternoon. Thoughts of

Papa's war stories inspired me to a new course of action. I spent many a winter's day listening to his tale about the attack on Trenton, the fear of the Hessian soldiers, and the ultimate knowledge that all he could do was press on in the face of his potential death. George Washington and Thomas Mifflin led their men to victory on that day, and while I do not have such noble allies, I do have my papa's willpower. I will not die waiting for this beast to find me in a pantry, cowering in fear.

August 13th, 1792

All my preparations have been completed. I have left a good amount of black powder under the window with the broken shutters. I trailed a small line to the doorway, where I will hide and add a flame to the powder when I see my hunter. If that fails, I have loaded papa's musket, and I found his flintlock pistol as well. I will have two shots at it if I am careful. Lastly, I have Papa's pitchfork. He told me he had once skewered a charging boar with it. I can only hope he was not telling me a tall tale.

I do not expect the house to survive the fight. As such, I have set all my money and some valuables in a trunk outside. I plan to wrap this journal up and lock it in a small box after I finish this entry. I will leave the key on top. That way, there will be a record of my life, and if someone comes looking for me, they'll find it. I am praying that I will be able to add another entry in the morning.

***

That was the last page. Part of me wondered if my co-workers had managed to pull a joke over on me. No way this was real. Right? I planned to bring the subject up at work the next day, but I never made it. That night, I was drifting to sleep when I heard glass shatter downstairs. I'm no wuss, so I grabbed my baseball bat and headed toward the sound. At the bottom of the steps, I spotted…well, I don't know what.

It had a long serpentine neck. Instead of a head, there was a giant boney needle that echoed suction-like sounds. Behind it's back were insectoid wings, it walked on two legs, but six rib-like appendages stuck out of its body. They opened and closed. In an instant, my brain filled in the picture. Those things were for holding prey tight while it drank from them with its needle neck. A small slit opened in its chest with a squishy pop, and out shot a short three-fingered claw, for pulling in the things it wanted to suck dry.

It's embarrassing to admit, and I never thought things like this really happened, but I pissed myself right there. I've been in enough scrapes to know that when it comes to fight or flight, my instinct is to fight, but the inhumanity of this thing short-circuited my brain. I fell backward and scrambled into my bedroom as it took a step up the stairs. Once I'd slammed the door shut, I shoved my dresser in front of it along with my bed for good measure. There were a series of scrapes outside the door, and I called the cops without knowing what else to do. I didn't own anything more offensive than the bat.

Of course, the police didn't believe a word of my story. They assumed I'd been high or hallucinated the monster. They even suggested I get a psych evaluation, but they couldn't deny the broken glass. They had a cop hang out for the rest of the night and advised me to get my window fixed.

The next day, I took off work and went to the library. I hadn't been there since a school trip in the fourth grade, but I knew they had smart people, librarians. Thankfully, Carolyn at the front desk knew all about Hazel Peak's older legends. I described the journal, but not my nighttime experience, and she said it might be related to the Night Terrors of 1792.

According to her, residents traced the origin of the incidents to the local Lenape. Many early Pennsylvanian's blamed Native Americans for everything that went wrong for them. This was especially true in Hazel Peak because the local tribe sided with the British in the Revolution. Carolyn also noted that some people were convinced the horrible events were connected to strange lights spotted in the sky for a week that year. She showed me a local artist's interpretation, it looked kind of like an aurora. I've seen them on that learning channel show where people have to survive in harsh climates. Except this aurora was purple and yellow. Carolyn said the color was probably the artist's creative interpretation.

Anyway, long story short, after the lights, a series of gruesome deaths started around the town, in the farms. People in Hazel Peak started to shun all farmers in the area because they feared the deaths were caused by some kind of disease spread by touch. Then all of a sudden, the deaths stopped in August. No one figured out how or why. No one wanted to go near the dead bodies to try and get an answer. The farms of the deceased were just burned up, and the people in town moved on. Carolyn gave me one last bit of unexpected information.

We went into a musty part of the library where old records are kept. While reviewing a history of the town's census information, she showed me that a woman named Ursula was listed as the wife of a new sheriff named Oscar Wagner in 1800. She had a family in 1810 and lived to be near eighty, as far as the records Carolyn could find told us.

I haven't quite figured out what I am going to do if the thing comes back. I could go buy a rifle and try to hold it off. If a sixteen-year-old girl killed whatever this is in 1790, surely, I can, right? But why did my discovery of the journal bring this creature back? Has it been hibernating since Ursula defeated it? Or was Ursula Wagner a different woman entirely? All I can think is that the journal contaminated me somehow. I am going to dispose of it. Then I'm going to figure out how to handle this thing. I just hope that Carolyn, my co-workers, and the police who came to my house aren't on the thing's radar now. I did my best to avoid touching people after I read the journal and saw the creature, but I can't be entirely certain I didn't graze any of them.

Monster in the Mine

"Why do you think this town has experienced so much tragedy?" My brother asks.

"Well, that's kind of a complicated question. Isn't it?"

"No. It's not. There's a monster that lives under the town. It fuels the cycles of violence here."

"A monster?"

"You're talking to a ghost, and the idea of a monster is unbelievable?"

I glance down to see where my brother's waist tapers into a misty cloud. Bits of ectoplasm drip off him and dissolve on contact with the floor. His upper half is how I remember it, sans clothing, but I can see through him to my closed bedroom door.

He floats to the window. "It lives in the abandoned mine underneath the town, inside the Gates of Hell. If you end its life, the spirits who've suffered from the violence it inspired will be able to rest. You can get revenge for me."

I sit up in bed. "How would I even kill a monster?"

"With a gun."

The door opens. My mom, dressed in her floral, green pajamas, stands in the doorway. Dark shadows color the skin under her eyes. My brother vanishes as she flicks on my bedroom light.

"Who are you talking to, Nate?" She asks.

"No one," I lie.

"You know it's okay if you're talking to Evan. I talk to him sometimes too." Mom walks to the edge of my bed and sits. "No one blames you for what happened."

I let out a frustrated sigh, lie back down, and turn away from her.

"It was cold that day, and your brother shouldn't have let you drive that route with only your learner's permit. Everyone knew how dangerous that hill could be in the winter, and we both know it's my fault for sending him to pick you up instead of doing it myself. I'm who you should blame."

I smell the alcohol on her breath, and I just want her to leave. "It's nobody's fault. The brake lines snapped in the cold. No one could've known what was going to happen."

Mom remains sitting on the bed, but I don't turn back to face her. I stare at the wall. Finally, she shuffles to the door, turns the light off, and leaves.

Evan reappears. "It's been a year, and she's still not back to normal?"

I keep my response low so that Mom doesn't pop back in. "You think losing your firstborn is easy to handle?"

"No, but she still has you to take care of. She can't afford to drown her sorrows at the bar every night."

"Why can't you appear to her? Knowing you still exist would help."

"Don't you think I've tried? She doesn't see me. You're the only one who can. I think it's because you watched me die."

My mind flashes back to Evan sitting next to me in the car. His head hangs limply from his body, and his last breaths come out in ragged, choking gasps. I'd reversed our vehicle into a snowbank when the brake lines snapped on the hill. If I hadn't steered us into the snow, our car would've crashed into the houses at the bottom of the incline. The impact crumpled his side of the vehicle while I only sustained minor scrapes and bruises.

"You were killed in a car accident. How was the monster responsible for that?"

"Didn't you ever wonder why the mechanic who inspected our car failed to notice the faulty brake line? He was old Hazel Peak stock, and he hated us because we weren't. The monster's influence ensures people give in to their worst instincts. This place is rotten to the core because of that thing's psychic emanations. Why don't you check out a history book if you don't believe me?"

I open my mouth to respond, but Evan vanishes.

***

The next day I am standing in the Hazel Peak Library. A musty smell lingers in the air. There are countless books, but I

53

have no idea which to review. I crouch down while trying to read some titles related to history.

"Need help?" A middle-aged woman with graying hair and a stack of books stands in the aisle. The t-shirt under her navy blazer displays a book cover for Aldous Huxley's *Brave New World*. The badge hanging from her hip displays her name, Carolyn.

"Yes, but I don't know what I'm looking for. I guess I need historical examples of bad things that happened in Hazel Peak?" I think about how odd that sounds and add, "It's for a history assignment."

Carolyn shelves one of the books from her stack. "Well, I've read a fair bit of Hazel Peak history. I can give you some examples, and maybe they can point you in the right direction?"

"That would be amazing."

"Do you mind following me as I work?"

"Not at all."

Carolyn moves down the aisle, putting books away. "Here's the first historical event I learned about Hazel Peak, and I think it sets the tone for all the rest. Soldiers under the command of George Washington came to the area to scout for Native Americans who'd allied with the British during the Revolutionary War. Unfortunately for the soldiers, the Native Americans knew the area far better than they did. When the soldiers made camp one evening, the Native Americans struck and killed everyone they could find. When families arrived to bury their dead, they discovered that the area was rather beautiful, aside from the blood-soaked soil. They were Hazel Peak's first settlers, and they proceeded to retaliate against every Native American to come through the area, regardless of whether they'd contributed to the initial attack. So, you can see the town began with violence."

"But we haven't had any major issues since then, right?" I ask, following her as she works.

"Unfortunately, we have." Carolyn frowns. "An influx of immigrant miners caused the town to swell in the late 1800s, but the newcomers suffered through horrible working conditions. They were underground all day and in debt to the mine companies for their supplies and homes. You can see why they unionized and went on strike." Carolyn moves to a new aisle, where another stack of books waits to be put away. "When the workers finally marched for better conditions, the mine owners hired Pinkertons, essentially rent-a-cops, to put a stop to it. They went after the marchers and unloaded on them with rifles. Eleven people were killed, and several were wounded. The newspapers called it the Mine March Massacre. Afterward, the Pinkertons wore disguises to their court date. As ridiculous as it sounds, the tactic worked because the witnesses who were shot at couldn't positively identify any of the shooters."

"That's insane. But nothing recent, right?" I ask.

"Last big tragedy was in the 1970s. The Mafia firebombed a family by mistake when they were trying to intimidate a Sheriff who lived next door. Since then, it's been relatively quiet. Although I've been told our crime statistics are higher than most towns."

I assist the librarian by handing her books from the nearest stack. "I have one last question, but it's going to be a weird one."

"What's that?" Carolyn stops shelving and stares at me.

"Have you ever heard about any monsters, like non-human ones, in Hazel Peak?"

I expect her to laugh, walk away, or sneer.

"A few rumblings. There was a gentleman in here a few years back saying he'd seen something he couldn't explain and asking about the town's history, kind of like you. I filled him in on the Night Terrors of 1792, when several local farmers mysteriously died in the area. Some blamed Native Americans and some thought bright lights in the sky were to blame."

I felt hope surge through me. "Can you give me that guy's phone number?"

"I'm afraid I don't have any contact details for him, he wasn't a regular member of the library, and I haven't seen him since."

"Well, thanks for all the information."

Carolyn smiles and nods. "I love getting to help people learn. It's one of the perks of being a librarian. Follow me. I'll write down some titles for you to check out on the subjects we discussed."

I walk with her to the front desk.

She jots down several book names on a sticky note and hands it to me. "If you need anything else, come find me."

"Thanks. I really appreciate it." I take the list and head back to the history section to find the recommended books.

**

After three hours of skimming the books from the library, I've confirmed everything Carolyn told me, and I've discovered a few extra tragedies she hadn't mentioned. The only topic I haven't found more information about is the monster itself. Aside from mentions of missing farmers in 1792, that subject is a dead end.

I'm sitting on my bed at home when Evan reappears.

"Where do I get a gun?" I ask.

"Mom keeps one in a safe under her bed. The key is in her nightstand drawer." Evan floats near the window.

"I never knew she had a gun."

"It was Dad's before he left. She just never got rid of it. You remember how to shoot from those times I took you out with my friends, right?"

"Yes. You made me go eight times the summer before…" I can't finish the statement, so I pivot to a new one. "Okay, I grab the gun, our butcher knife, some other supplies, and I head for the Gates of Hell. What then?"

Evan mimes shooting a gun. "It won't take you long to find the creature. It stays close to the exit to come out and eat its victims."

"And you're sure a seventeen-year-old with a gun is going to be able to kill it?"

"It's not a physically strong creature. If you don't do this, the spirits who've died in Hazel Peak because of its cycles of violence will continue to suffer spiritual torment. Don't you want us to be able to rest in peace?"

"Yes. I've just never done anything like this." I stand up. "What if you're just in my head? How do I know you're not some manifestation of my grief?" I push my fist into Evan's chest. My fingers are cold, and the hairs on my arm stick up.

"I can prove it without you needing to catch a chill." Evan floats over to my desk. He reaches down to a pencil I'd left out after doing my math homework. His hand becomes more substantial for a moment, and he picks the item up. The writing utensil hovers in the air. Evan's form shimmers in and out of existence before fading to the barest hint of an outline as the pencil drops to the floor. "Interacting with the world is possible for me, but it drains my essence to the point where you won't be able to see me again until I recover. I'll still be here watching you, though." Evan vanishes.

I walk over to my desk, bend over, and pick up the pencil. It feels like I'm clutching an icicle. The thought of my brother watching me while I can't perceive him gives me a shiver, but my doubts are gone.

I leave my bedroom and head to my mom's room. It's a mess inside, with clothes piled along her dresser. Two stale beers sit on her nightstand. I open the top drawer and sort through takeout menus, makeup items, and cigarettes. The key Evan told me about sits at the bottom. I take it and drop to the floor. There's a small, gray safe, one step up from a lockbox, pushed to the furthest point under the mattress. Evan is right again. I haul it out, unlock it, and find a gun that looks like it's been tossed out of a Western. It's a black revolver with a wood grip. I take the weapon and the small box of ammo. The gun's metal is cold to the touch, reminding me of my disembodied brother. I restore things to how they were before my intrusion and return to my bedroom.

After hiding the gun, I venture around the house, stuffing my backpack with everything I think I'll need: Duct tape, just in case, Granola bars, for energy, and my water bottle, for hydration. In the kitchen, I slide a drawer open and remove our largest knife. It's a white ceramic blade that Evan got my mom for Christmas three years ago. He'd broken her best knife trying to pry apart an old television with his friends, and this had been his apology. I put the knife in the bag. Lastly, I dig out my old flashlight and find working batteries for it in our junk cabinet.

When I'm satisfied with my supplies, I sit down at my computer and look up videos about improving my target accuracy, operating a revolver, and navigating old mines.

***

It's noon on Sunday when I arrive at the Gates of Hell.

The mine entrance is a dark maw carved out of the side of a mountain. A torn-down chain-link fence lies before it. Mom had told me the location got its name when the remains of a chicken set inside a chalk-drawn pentagram were found outside the tunnel in the eighties. The resulting Satanic panic led to the town erecting a fence, which teenagers quickly destroyed. Autumn's winds have removed leaves from most of the surrounding trees.

I swing my backpack down, pull out my flashlight, the gun, the knife, and my ammo. Muscle memory comes back quickly, and I pop the revolver's chamber and load six shells. I store the left-over bullets in the bag, and I slide the knife into my front pocket for easy reach. Prepped, I return the bag to my back and start forward with a gun in my right hand and a switched-on flashlight in my left.

With a deep breath, I scramble over the downed fence and proceed into the darkness ahead. The walls are smoothly tunneled out, and I have plenty of room to walk. At my feet are the remnants of an old cart track. My hope is that there's nothing in here to find, and my ghostly brother was mistaken about the monster.

The air is warm at first, but when I can no longer see the sun behind me, a cool breeze from within the mine starts to give me goosebumps. I look for signs of any living thing in the flashlight's beams. Every step I take echoes through the tunnel, and there's a steady drip of water coming from somewhere. A rancid, rotten smell slithers its way into my nostrils, but I continue forward. Ahead, the path splits. Something out of place in the tunnel to the left catches my attention.

I move that direction, and the light reveals a pile of bones.

A shudder runs through my body. There aren't enough recognizable pieces to identify the supplying creature. More skeletal parts lead deeper into the mine. It's practically a trail of breadcrumbs. I keep the gun held tight and aimed forward as I advance.

It's hard not to step on the bones as they start to clutter the entire path. The horrid stench grows stronger. There's a loud crunch as I shatter old bones beneath my feet. A solitary light, in the shape of a triangle, comes to life in the distance. My heart's beating turns frantic. Something knows I'm here.

I continue forward, ready to face the monster. The wealth of bones grows to ridiculous proportions around my feet. I spot several human skulls amongst the macabre debris.

The tunnel's walls cease abruptly as I enter a cavernous space. As I step closer, I realize the triangular light ahead is a teepee radiating luminosity from within. The pale pigmentation of the teepee's material reminds me of human skin, and a thin figure is silhouetted inside. Whatever is in there has an elongated cranium and two spindly arms.

The head swivels in my direction. "I caught a whiff of your blood as soon as you entered the mine. I'd hoped the skeletons would dissuade you, but you kept coming." The voice emanating from the darkened profile is cold and raspy. "You must have a purpose here. What is it?"

I raise my weapon and aim at the teepee.

"Is that gun oil I smell? You're here for me?"

My finger starts squeezing the trigger back to fire.

"Please, don't."

The plea startles me into halting my shot.

"Why do you want to kill me? Can we talk first?"

My mouth is as dry as sandpaper, but I manage a reply. "Yes."

"What harm have I done you?"

"You killed my brother."

The shadowy figure adjusts its position inside the teepee. "I've never killed a living thing."

I almost laugh. "How do you explain all these bones?"

"All these organisms were dead before I consumed their flesh for sustenance and used what I needed to make this home."

"My brother told me you fuel the cycles of violence in Hazel Peak. You keep people's spirits in agony."

"I thought you said your brother was dead?"

The gun feels heavy in my hand from holding it up for so long. "He is, but his ghost told me everything I needed to know."

"Ghost? There is no such thing." The teepee's illumination fades to nothing.

"What're you doing? Why'd you put the light out?"

The only answer is a tearing sound, and I realize the speaker is trying to escape out the back of the dwelling. Adrenaline surges through me, and I circumvent the teepee. As I reach the other side, my flashlight reveals a hole in the lining at eye level. The noxious scent from earlier oozes out of the opening. Two hands, with six long, boney protrusions, retract back into the teepee's darkness. My light reflects off something scarlet within.

"Human, I've done you no harm. Let me go."

"Even if you only eat the dead, that doesn't mean you aren't causing this town's violence."

The monster cackles. "A series of complex human interactions, beliefs, and goals mix to create violent results throughout your history, and you think a single being is responsible? Your species needs a group or person to persecute at all times, and when you don't have one, you'll find a scapegoat, like me."

Evan appears in a burst of radiant azure. "Don't believe its lies. The monster is to blame for the evil in Hazel Peak."

I jump in shock, but I'm happy to see my brother.

The monster whispers through the torn hole, "I can hear that ghost too, you know, and while I've never found evidence of human souls living after death, there are other beings, hungry things, that live in the dark. They want into this world. I keep some at bay, and they fear me. They want me gone. I've never known them to take human guise before, but there's a first time for everything. You're being used."

Evan floats to my side. "More lies. It's not even human. You've got to kill it and end the violence. Free our souls!"

The gun trembles in my grasp. All the words I've heard swim through my mind. Evan smiles and nods for me to get on with the shooting. I picture his head hanging limply in the passenger seat again. I owe him for taking his life with my stupid driving. Tears well up in my eyes. I fire.

The first shot pierces the teepee, and the monster lets out an agonized wail. The structure rips apart as I fire again. The creature is cloaked by shadows and tatters, but I catch a glimpse of a gray, worm-like lower body slithering inside. I pull the trigger a third time. The shot ricochets off some rocks and bounces around the space, making it impossible to hear anything else. Two boney claws slash toward me as the monster frees itself of its shredded living area and charges.

Atop its head is a single, crimson eye, and its mouth is open wide, revealing rows of vicious, jagged teeth. I pull the trigger as fast as I can, firing my final bullets in rapid succession. Black ichor spills out from its midsection as two holes appear in its flesh. The monster is still coming, and its claws connect with my hands, sending my gun flying into the darkness and my flashlight skittering to the ground.

I scramble to pull my knife out while backing away from the monster. The flashlight spins where it landed nearby. I get a grip on my weapon. One second, the approaching form is illuminated, and in the next, we're both in darkness. I hear the monster sliding over the rocky floor and my breath coming in quick bursts. The light swivels around again to reveal the creature within arm's reach. I see the wormy lower body, the spindly arms, and the freakish head. The alienness disgusts me. I pull back my knife and prepare to strike.

"Please," it says. "Don't. I want to liv—"

My knife plunges through the monster's eye.

Regret surges through me as the thing slides back off my blade and collapses to the ground, dead. Its blood flows out to form a pool around its foreign form. My knife drips with its vital fluids. Mercifully, the light stops spinning and keeps the creature's corpse shrouded in darkness. I look for my brother, but he's gone. The monster's last words echo in my head.

I collect my flashlight and search for my gun. As I explore the area, I'm careful to avoid the spot where the monster fell. I don't want another glimpse of what I did to it. The pistol lies at the edge of the ruined teepee. Inside the dwelling, there is an extinguished lantern and some half-eaten rabbits. My gun is scuffed from the ruckus, but I suspect my mom won't ever notice the mark.

As I turn to leave, I realize the monster's black blood has stained my white, ceramic knife. I'll have to buy a new one for the house and get rid of this one. I look back at the teepee in disbelief as I tuck the gun and ammo into my bag. If only Evan could appear again and tell me it had worked, and he was free, my actions would feel justified.

***

I add a newly purchased ceramic knife to our kitchen a week later. I'd also cleaned the gun before successfully returning it to my mom's safe. I'm still hoping she'll never notice the six missing bullets. I've struggled with nightmares of the mine every night since coming back. The last words of the monster continue to repeat in my brain, but I try to keep Evan's words there too. He'd said the thing lied.

Mom walks into the kitchen with a grim look on her face. "Oh, God. Did you hear the news?"

"What's up?"

"Some psychos just shot up a diner downtown. It's horrible. They live-streamed the whole thing, and it's all over social media. The cops got them, thank God, but I can't believe people would do something so sick." She goes to the fridge and pulls out a beer.

My body trembles. "But I stopped the monster."

Mom continues to search for a beer in the fridge. "What's that, Nate?"

Evan's ghost appears behind Mom. He smiles and winks at me. His spectral form begins to change. The upper body vanishes, and dozens of spidery appendages erupt from his elongating head as his eyes burst. His nostrils expand into cavernous holes, which consume most of Evan's remaining flesh. In their depths, legions of squirming, insectile figures scuttle for escape. Before the millions of carapaces erupt from the face, the apparition vanishes. There's a moment of relief before a thought shatters my mind.

I killed the monster that was keeping the hungry things at bay.

The Abyss Within

The following is a transcript of a recording recovered from the Hazel Peak autopsy of a John Doe. If you have any knowledge of what occurred, please contact the Hazel Peak Police Department. This transcript has not been edited in any way.

Medical Examiner (ME) Creed: "This is Hazel Peak Medical Examiner Creed starting the autopsy of an unidentified white male. Subject was delivered by Hazel Peak police after being found incapacitated outside school playground. According to police, subject was alive and talking about a 'shadow man' he met. Subject was pronounced dead by arriving EMTs. Cause of death is presumed to be a heart attack. Subject was wearing a suit upon arrival. Black pants, jacket, and a white dress shirt. Underneath were flannel boxers. Subject has no tattoos or piercings. Weight is approximately 320 pounds, and he measures six feet in length. Nothing of note regarding male genitalia and anus shows no sign of injury. Hair is graying brown, and eyes are dull blue. No facial hair. Rigor mortis is not yet present. Proceeding with examination of chest cavity.

Medical Assistant (MA) Shelly: "Doesn't the microphone hanging above the body ever get distracting?"

ME Creed: "You get used to it. Why don't you make the Y incision to get us started?"

MA Shelly: "Are you sure? I haven't been here that long."

ME Creed: "If you're going to take over for me one day then you'll need to start doing this kind of stuff."

MA Shelly: "Okay."

ME Creed: "Don't forget to narrate for the record."

MA Shelly: "Starting the incision. Cutting from the right shoulder to the middle of the chest. Now cutting down to the belly button. Struggling due to this guy's huge gut."

ME Creed: "Let's keep it respectful."

MA Shelly: "Sorry, this guy's, uh, enlarged intestinal area."

ME Creed: "Not bad. You'll get better as you go."

MA Shelly: "Completing Y incision with cut from left shoulder. Setting aside my scalpel and peeling back the subject's skin.

ME Creed: "Here, I'll help."

MA Shelly: "Thanks. Subject's rib cage is below. Should I get the saw?"

ME Creed: "Not until you've got your skin flap secured."

MA Shelly: "My mistake. Now I've got it."

ME Creed: "Good. Now you can start the saw. Remember to stop the saw before you try to narrate again."

MA Shelly: "Starting the saw now."

For a moment there is nothing but the sound of sawing.

MA Shelly: "Halfway cut, but there's something strange."

ME Creed: "Don't be shy. Put it on the record."

MA Shelly: "It feels like there is a draft coming from inside the body."

ME Creed: "I noticed a chill myself, but I doubt it came from the body. Our air conditioner probably kicked on while you were sawing."

MA Shelly: "That must be it. Resuming saw."

There is more sawing for another moment.

MA Shelly: "Sawing complete. Proceeding to remove the rib cage."

The sound of cracking occurs.

MA Shelly: "My god. Can you verify what I'm seeing?"

ME Creed: "I, it, it can't be."

MA Shelly: "Should we get someone else in here?"

ME Creed: "No. Not yet. Not until we know this isn't some kind of wild joke."

MA Shelly: "A joke?"

ME Creed: "Is there another plausible explanation?"

MA Shelly: "Help me try to get him on his side."

ME Creed: "Good idea."

MA Shelly: "Almost got him up. Damn."

ME Creed: "The table is all that appears under the subject. Good god, how is that possible?"

MA Shelly: "Let's drop him back down."

ME Creed: "I don't understand how it's possible."

MA Shelly: "Should we narrate it for the record?"

ME Creed: "Yes. I'll do it. Medical Assistant Shelly has just completed the removal of the subject's ribcage. Inside is, well, all of the subjects' organs are missing, and–"

MA Shelly: "And there's a fucking staircase leading down inside of this guy. It doesn't make any sense. And when I stick my arm inside the cavity it goes beyond the point where it should hit the table."

ME Creed: "What Medical Assistant Shelly says is accurate. The stairs appear to be some kind of black stone. They feel cold to the touch, and the chill Shelly previously noted is coming out of the staircase. I can't see the bottom. Can you?"

MA Shelly: "No, but it's so dark. I count fifteen stairs before I can't see anymore. Are you sure this isn't some kind of ritual hazing? The old, 'scare the new staff member with the MC Escher corpse' bit?"

ME Creed: "If only. Do you think one of us could fit inside."

MA Shelly: "You can't actually be considering going down those stairs."

ME Creed: "Well, I for one want to know what the hell is going on here."

MA Shelly: "Yeah, but why don't we get a police officer or someone to go down there? This isn't exactly in our job description."

ME Creed: "Maybe you're right."

Female Voice: "Jack, is that you? It's so dark down here. Jack?"

MA Shelly: "Holy Hell. Did you just hear someone shouting up from down there? Or was that in my head?"

Female Voice: "You're not Jack. Who's there?"

MA Shelly: "That's your name, isn't it? She's asking for you?"

ME Creed: "It's not possible. I know that voice."

MA Shelly: "None of this is possible. I'm sure we'll wake up at any moment. Who is it?"

ME Creed: "My wife."

MA Shelly: "But isn't she?"

ME Creed: "Dead. For eight years. Drunk driver sent her off a bridge."

Female Voice (now identified as Mrs. Creed): "Jack. I've got Emily down here. She's doing great now. Come down and see."

MA Shelly: "Wait, stop. What are you doing?"

ME Creed: "I have to go down there."

MA Shelly: "You're crazy, we need to call the police, or better yet, the FBI."

ME Creed: "No one but my wife knew the name we'd picked out for our unborn child."

MA Shelly: "Your wife died pregnant? I didn't know. I'm so sorry."

ME Creed: "I have to check if she's really down there."

MA Shelly: "I can't stop you, but I highly recommend you reconsider. Just think for a second. This is all insane. What are the chances your wife has returned from the grave with your unborn child inside a deceased stranger?"

Mrs. Creed: "Jack, it's so cold down here. And it's dark. I can hear you, but I can't find my way out. I need light. Emily needs you."

ME Creed: "I'm coming honey. Hold on. Shelly, hand me that flashlight."

MA Shelly: "Here. But be careful. Do you need anything else from me?"

ME Creed: "Just stay here in case I need you to throw something down. For the record, I'm climbing atop the man and squeezing inside the cavity now."

MA Shelly: "I'm going to keep talking because I don't know what the hell else to do. Jack, er, Medical Examiner Creed is descending the stairs inside the corpse. I can see his light growing dimmer. Are you okay, so far?"

ME Creed: "Yes, nothing to report yet. Just stairs. Honey? Are you near?"

Mrs. Creed: "I can see your light. You're almost to me."

MA Shelly: "Medical Examiner Creed's light just vanished abruptly. Sir? Jack?"

ME Creed: "It's fine down here Shelly. Come down. You won't believe it."

MA Shelly: "I already don't believe it. I don't need to come down there. Why don't you come up?"

ME Creed: "I need another light. Please, bring me one."

MA Shelly: "I can toss one down. Wouldn't that be good enough?"

ME Creed: "It would break. Please. Help me get my wife and child out of here."

Mrs. Creed: "Help us."

MA Shelly: "No. I can't. It's too weird for me."

ME Creed: "You're going to let me and my family remain lost in the dark down here?"

MA Shelly: "I, okay, I'm coming down, but I'll meet you halfway. I'm not going to the bottom of the stairs. I'm just going to the edge of the light."

ME Creed: "That's fine. That'll work."

MA Shelly: "I'm crawling inside the body now. Descending the stairs. I'm stopped on the fifteenth stair. Can you see my light?"

ME Creed: "Yes, just wait there. Can't you see how grand it is down here?"

MA Shelly: "I don't see much of, wait, it's getting brighter. I can see walls. It's enormous down here. It's like a cavern. There's something white a few steps below me. Did you notice that on your way down Jack?"

Mrs. Creed: "Jack fell. We need you to come down further. I can't support him without you."

MA Shelly: "No. I'm going back up now. I won't come down any further. The light is brighter now. I can almost make out whatever is on the steps, it looks like, oh my god."

Mrs. Creed: "Join us down here in the dark. We need company."

ME Creed: "Come on Shelly, it feels marvelous."

MA Shelly: "You can't be. I'm staring at what's left of your—the body's chest cavity is closing above me. No. Help!"

Silence reigns for a long moment.

Secretary: "Jack, do you and the newbie want me to order lunch? Jack?"

After several hours, Medical Examiner Creed's secretary reported him and his assistant missing. A search of the facility discovered nothing out of place. The John Doe's corpse remained on the table with the ribcage removed. The organs were present inside. An additional examination revealed the man died of a heart attack, as assumed. The body remains unidentified, and the medical examiner and his assistant remain missing.

Seven Entries in The Midnight Path

Evidence Identification Number 03051970 – 09/13/2019 – 12:00 P.M. – The journal below was written by Ms. Jennifer Tillinghast. Ms. Tillinghast vanished amidst an outbreak of violence at the Board Game Coffee House on 03/13/2015. Ms. Tillinghast was previously sought for questioning in relation to the murder of Lisa Barron, the lover of her ex-husband, Kevin Upton. Ms. Tillinghast's journal was found in a gas station near Bird City, Kansas, and forwarded to the Hazel Peak Police Department by Kansas Highway Patrol. Ms. Tillinghast's former psychologist, Dr. Kiste, has made notes between the journal entries to provide greater insight into Ms. Tillinghast's thinking.

Entry 1 – Saturday, March 7th

My therapist suggested I start journaling. Her instructions were to record a day and then flip the page and forget about it. I'm only supposed to review my scribblings at the end of the week. Hopefully, I'll see some healing progress in the tapestry of journal entries. It's all supposed to help me move past the incident, although she objects to my name for that day. She says I'm empowering the event, but I can't seem to find a better word for "the day you got a text message meant for your husband's fuckbuddy." Incident works fine for me.

Whatever you want to call that day, I've been solo since. Readjusting to living alone has been strange after five years of cohabitation. At first, I was almost happy. There wasn't anyone leaving dirty dishes in the sink, losing things around the house, or distracting me from reading, but I've been lonely the last few days.

The highlight of my first day journaling was finding an old book called *The Midnight Path* down at Cupboard Books. I've always been fascinated by occultists like Aleister Crowley, and this book is the autobiography of one of his peers. The man's name was Jean Tremblay. He was born in France, but he ended up moving across the English Channel before finding his way into Crowley's circle for a time. Eventually, he ended up residing in New York City. There, Jean grew in magical reputation until famous residents were visiting him. The entirety of Tammany Hall was rumored to attend his monthly parties at the Chelsea Hotel. During the height of his notoriety in 1925, he vanished.

The Midnight Path was found six decades later in a gas station near Bird City, Kansas. Extensive handwriting analysis established the autobiography as authentic, and the book was quickly reprinted by an enterprising small press. Unfortunately, the satanic panic killed any market for the book, and the print run ended up extremely small. All of this is what I remember from the Wikipedia page, but I've always found the topic fascinating, and I was toying with creating a board game based on the subject. It might give me something to do with all my newfound free time. I'm going to try and start reading the book tonight.

Until tomorrow,

J. T.

Dr. Kiste's Notes: Jennifer's situation was not uncommon. I have dealt with many wives who have had cheating husbands. The exercise I assigned was intended to allow Jennifer to work through her feelings and provide the distance for her to reassess her emotions once the week elapsed. Past patients have responded extraordinarily well to this undertaking. Based on this first entry, I don't see any issues in Jennifer's thinking. I should note that Jennifer's journal being found in the same location as the original version of *The Midnight Path* is unlikely to have been a coincidence. I assume Jennifer left this journal there intentionally.

Entry 2 – Sunday, March 8th

I can't help thinking about what my ex-husband might be doing. As much as I hate that he cheated on me for weeks, I still miss the couple's shorthand we hand. The way I could give him a look and communicate how annoyed I was with our mutual friend Carol's latest boy drama. The way he could grab my thigh in just the right spot to let me know he wanted to screw. The sex was great, and what's horrible is that I noticed how exciting it'd gotten during the time he was cheating on me. He was trying all these new moves in the bedroom, and I loved them. It was only after I found out about Lisa that I realized where they were coming from. Now thinking about our sex life makes me want to puke.

Today's been tough. I've been dwelling way too much. I took some time off work to focus on some of my hobbies, relax, and get over Kevin, but I'm quickly realizing all this time alone is a bad idea. Maybe I'll take a trip to grab a good hoagie from that pizza shop downtown tomorrow? They make the best food. This probably isn't the kind of thing my therapist wants me writing in here, but hey, it's my journal.

Here's something weird. I found a copy of *The Midnight Path* on my bedside table this morning. I've heard about the book before, and I've always wanted to review a copy, but I have no clue how this got here. Maybe it's a parting gift from Kevin? He does still have a key to the house. Anyway, the book was written by an occultist, and he vanished under mysterious circumstances before this autobiography appeared years later. Spooky stuff. So, naturally, I can't wait to read it. Maybe I'll dive into the pages tonight. It should make for some good bedtime reading.

Until tomorrow,

J.T.

Dr. Kiste's Notes: It is not uncommon for spouses who have been cheated on to still want their partner back. It is a little surprising how open Jennifer is about her sex life above as she would not speak about it in our sessions. This is a significant reason why the journaling exercise is successful. It makes patients discuss their issues as if no one is listening. Of course, the most severe red flag in this entry is that Jennifer has forgotten that she bought *The Midnight Path* the day prior. This is a sign that the stresses of her divorce were more significant than I initially realized.

Entry 3 – Monday, March 9th

Went to the pizza shop, Two Uncles, and got an Italian hoagie today. Tasted great. They make the best subs. The bread is shipped in from somewhere special. Philadelphia maybe? Does Philadelphia have good bread? Anyway, while I was there, the owner asked how my husband was doing. I stammered through an awkward explanation the guy didn't need. I could've gotten out of there with a simple "we split up." Instead, I gave him the whole story. By the time I was done recounting everything, there was a line of people jammed behind me. Completely embarrassing. Why am I so awkward? Ironically, the one person who'd understand this is Kevin. I want to call him, but I can't help feeling like he'd win the battle of wills if I did that. He messed up, and he should be the one to come back to me. He won't, of course.

Since I got home, I've been endeavoring to forget the Two Uncles fiasco. I started working on a board game based on this occultist I always found fascinating, Jean Tremblay. Kevin introduced me to board games, but I went crazy for them, whereas he lost interest. Making my own game has been a dream of mine for a while now. I don't feel like writing Tremblay's entire backstory in my journal, but he's an interesting historical figure. The game puts players in his disciples' shoes, trying to curry his favor, learn spells, and pay off corrupt New York City politicians.

If players learn too many evil spells, they start to become tainted by darkness, which means they spend the rest of the game being hunted by the Midnight God. They need to use magic points to keep the creature off their trail.

Well, that's just a rough outline of the game. I started assembling my prototype today. It's all based on real-life occultism, specifically Tremblay's beliefs. I was inspired to start working on the game when I found his autobiography, *The Midnight Path*, on my front doorstep. I must've bought a copy online recently, but I can't recall when. Things have been crazy with the divorce, so this could've slipped my mind. That said, I would love to figure out the company that shipped the book to me because it was beaten up. There are scorch marks and scratches all over it. Regardless, I'm planning to dive into this for my evening's reading.

Until tomorrow,

J.T.

Dr. Kiste's Notes: In this entry, I was happy that Jennifer gave herself a project to focus on. Unfortunately, her memory issue continues. I can only posit that Jennifer was the person responsible for damaging her copy of *The Midnight Path* during the previous night.

Entry 4 – Tuesday, March 10th

Three days gone, and I've avoided looking back at any of my past entries. I can't say it's been that hard so far. Anyway, I'm feeling good now. I'm not going to pretend I haven't thought about Kevin on and off, but my thoughts about him felt a little less dire today.

I continued to tinker on my board game today. *The Midnight Path* is developing into quite a compelling little project. I might bring it out to the Board Game Coffee House for a playtest soon. The owner is super friendly, and he's great about encouraging new game designers with tips. I never could've done as much work on a project like this if my husband was still here. He always distracted me from my passions. Now I'm free to do what I want when I want. Although, I can't blame anyone else when something's wrong in the house now.

The front door was open when I woke up today. It wasn't swinging in the wind or anything like that, but it was open a fair crack. I spent the early part of the day looking for any critters that might've gotten in overnight. No idea how I managed to leave it open like that. Reminds me of the time I left my car running all night. Unlike that instance, I don't have any drugs to thank for this mistake.

One good thing did come out of the error though. While I was poking around the house, I found my small, locked safe under my bed. I always kept it in the closet, and I don't know how it got moved under the bed. When I opened it, I found a stack of papers I'd never seen before. At first, I was a little freaked out, but then I remembered Kevin used to have a key to the safe too. He must've moved it and hidden these in there before he killed our relationship.

As far as I can tell, the papers are from the autobiography of Jean Tremblay, the guy whose life I'm basing my board game off. Kevin must've intended to bind them and give them to me for my birthday. I know I should probably feel sad to have found a lost present from my ex-husband, but I'm just so excited to get to read this. Copies are incredibly hard to find. I remember coming across one in Cupboard Books at some point in the past. I can't remember why I didn't pick it up at the time. Well, I'm spending my night reading this.

Until tomorrow,

J.T.

Dr. Kiste's Notes: It is exceptionally odd that Jennifer remembers working on a board game based on Jean Tremblay's work, but she cannot recall buying his book. There are also suggestions that Jennifer was having some sort of intense nighttime episodes. It appears that *The Midnight Path* was seriously worsened from its condition the previous night.

Entry 5 – Wednesday, March 11th

It's raining outside today. I've only managed to make it from my bed to the couch. Kevin would always talk me off the ledge when I fell into these moods before. Now, I've got no one to call. I left all my friendships on the side of the road when things got serious with the lost love. This serves me right, I guess.

I thought about tinkering with my board game, but I found it smashed to pieces. I'm not sure what the hell happened to it. Maybe an earthquake in the night? Big gust of wind? My own shoddy craftsmanship? I don't think Kevin is so vindictive that he'd break in just to smash something that was bringing me joy. At least, I hope he isn't. Probably for the best anyway. It was a complicated game. Who was I kidding? Why did I think I had any talent or ability to make something anyone else would enjoy? I'm destined to stay working in an office as a wage slave until I drop dead.

This world tells you that you can do whatever you want, but that's bullshit. You can only go as far as your family's status and wealth will allow. Born middle class? Tough luck, you'll be working a menial job until you drop dead to pay for the college degree you needed to get the menial job. It's all one big trap, and I can't help thinking we deserve a button to stop the ride and let ourselves off.

Fuck. I miss Kevin. Why did he cheat on me? Did he tire of being with someone who wasn't a bubbly, cookie-cutter member of consumer society?

I guess the only thing of interest that I can write about today, besides the black hole in my chest swallowing my happiness, is the fact that I found a few scattered pages of a book near the couch. I think they might be excerpts from the autobiography I was basing my board game on, *The Midnight Path* by Jean Tremblay. I'm not entirely sure yet, but if I can get myself off the couch, I will try to see if there are more pages around. The only weird thing about this is that I don't remember ever owning or bringing home anything related to that book. It's ridiculously hard to find. Maybe I'll call Kevin today, just to make sure he didn't stop by and drop it off without me realizing.

Until tomorrow,

J.T.

Dr. Kiste's Notes: Here, Jennifer slips into a depression. It appears her already fragile mood is impacted by the weather. Once again, Jennifer seems to have tried to harm *The Midnight Path* between entries and forgot she owned it. It's not impossible that Jennifer wrote this journal with the intention of confusing those who read it, but my opinion is that she was suffering through nightly fugue states.

Entry 6 – Thursday, March 12th

Well, per my therapist's instruction, this is the last entry I need to record before reviewing the previous pages to look for catharsis. Tomorrow, expect me to write something profound about what this breakup has meant. While I know I've still got a long way to go, I'm feeling better today than yesterday.

I woke up on the couch around midnight and realized I'd wasted my entire day feeling miserable. Time is the one thing you really can't get back in this life. It's the one personal resource we shouldn't undervalue. So, when I woke up in the middle of the night, I brewed some coffee and went about setting things right.

First, I rebuilt my board game. I even made some excellent modifications to it. I think people will really respond to this version. Then, I quit my job. Yeah, I know it's a bold step, but I just can't go back to that place and act like a drone for the rest of my life. Game designing is my passion, and I will sink or swim in that field. Lastly, when the morning arrived, I gave Kevin a call. I know. Not a good idea.

But the conversation was amicable, and I think enough time had passed that we were able to really discuss what happened. He said my anger and depression at where I was in life had started to rub off on him. I apologized. Oddly, the conversation took a sexual turn near the end. He told me Lisa didn't please him, and he was really missing our time together. I was advised to make these entries entirely honest, so I'll admit that I met up with Kevin this afternoon, and we were intimate. God, it hadn't been that great since we'd first met. And I felt so empowered knowing that he was now cheating with me.

Afterward, I even showed Kevin my game. He loved it. He's never loved any of my projects before. After playing, Kevin seemed different somehow. Calmer maybe? I asked what our fling meant, and he told me he planned to end things with Lisa and return tomorrow.

I've won him back, and he won't leave me again. Not after everything we've gone through. He's even agreed to support me while I create games. It's going to be better than ever.

I spent the rest of the day cleaning up the house in preparation for his return. Thankfully, I hadn't yet thrown out any of the stuff he'd failed to take with him when he left. I restored it all to its rightful place. In the process of cleaning up the house, I collected a ton of pages from a book I think might be *The Midnight Path*, the basis of my board game. I have no idea how they ended up in my house, but I'm attempting to reassemble them. There are burn marks on some of the pages, and a few are cut up. It looks like someone went through a lot of effort to wreck and scatter these throughout my home, but I've been here for a week and haven't noticed any signs of a break-in. Why would someone risk jail just to hide ruined pages anyway?

Since Kevin and I were back on good terms, I called him about the book scraps. He told me I needed to read through the pages. Kevin said the game I'd made managed to convey the book's message to him, but I needed to fully understand it myself. I was a bit perplexed, but I loved that he suddenly shared my passion for Jean Tremblay. So, I'm stapling this book back together and diving into it tonight.

Until tomorrow,

J.T.

Dr. Kiste's Notes: This entry is exciting to start with because Jennifer seems to have come out of her depression ready to re-take control of her life. Unfortunately, reaching out to Kevin appears to have been a significant step backward on her road to recovering from the divorce. Kevin's actions are typical of a serial adulterer as he jumps at the chance to cheat on his current lover with his ex. It's odd that Jennifer didn't seem to have any negative feelings about this. Once again, Jean Tremblay's book appears as if Jennifer has no recollection of buying it. Furthermore, it seems as if she'd tried to violently exorcize the book from her life the night before. Jennifer's continued attempts to rationalize what is happening are extremely concerning. It appears she may have slipped into a severe delusion. As is popularly accepted, people with serious mental disorders don't often recognize that they have them, and this journal clearly illustrates Jennifer was unaware of her own growing instability. As to Kevin's newfound interest in Jean Tremblay, I believe he was lying to get back into the good graces of Jennifer.

Entry 7 – Friday, March 13th

What the fuck? I just reviewed my previous entries. I don't remember buying *The Midnight Path* in Cupboard Books. I don't remember ever trying to read it. Everything else in the pages is precisely what happened, but all my mentions of Jean Tremblay's book are total mysteries to me. Am I losing my mind? Was someone else breaking in and swapping my journal with a forged one? Could this have been Kevin's doing? I guess that would fit, considering what happened last night.

Kevin went back to Lisa after our time together, and he took a power drill to her left eyeball. He must've been having a breakdown for a while. His cheating could've been the first sign, and I completely missed it.

Of course, the cops seem suspicious of me. I'm sure they think we conspired to get Lisa out of the picture, but they aren't arresting me yet because Kevin made no attempt to conceal the murder. He apparently killed Lisa with the front door wide open, and the neighbors phoned the cops. Kevin didn't resist when the police arrived, but they said he looked like he was coming off a manic episode. I'd never noticed him having mood changes like that before. I was always the one whose emotions swung like an amusement park pirate ship. They think something snapped inside of him. Apparently, he kept babbling about my board game. I showed it to the cops and told them everything about our day yesterday. I even showed them my sixth journal entry. They said they'd be back soon with further questions, and they'll need to collect my journal and game as evidence. No way in hell I'm letting that happen. The game is the first thing I've ever made that anyone's liked.

So, I'm going to bring it straight to the Board Game Coffee House and get as many people as possible to playtest it. Jean Tremblay would want me to spread his message.

I'm shocked at how invigorated I feel by this decision and everything that's happened today. Lisa is dead, and Kevin will be locked up. A fitting end for a woman who took what wasn't hers and a husband who cheated.

I'm cured. The source of my pain is gone, and I have a new passion in my life. Hell, there are plenty of blank pages left here for me to start my own gospel. It will be the beginning of my own version of *The Midnight Path*.

Until tomorrow,

J.T.

Dr. Kiste's Notes: This entry is, of course, the most concerning. Initially, it appears Jennifer is facing the delusion she has created regarding her copy of *The Midnight Path*, but then she is consumed by it. Her excitement over Lisa's death shows latent sociopathic tendencies, and she appears to adopt Jean Tremblay as her personal prophet. It should be noted that this fascination with Jean Tremblay may be why she only wrote her name out as J.T. in the journal. Perhaps, she wanted to revel in the fact that she had the same initials as the object of her obsession. Of course, while this journal points to a deranged mind, it is unknown how Jennifer Tillinghast managed to convey her insanity to others. Six customers were killed by people who played her board game version of *The Midnight Path* on 03/13/2015. In addition, Jennifer and her game have yet to be located. Procuring and reading a copy of Jean Tremblay's *The Midnight Path* will allow me to gain further insight into Jennifer's mind. I have already ordered a copy to review.

Part 3

Demented Deities

Our King Needs Subjects

1

Christmas lights twinkle and bathe the apartment in a festive glow. Alice is in her reindeer pajamas, with her blonde hair up in a ponytail, and Robert wears a white t-shirt and boxers, with stubble covering his jaw. They sit, enjoying the scented cinnamon sticks hanging from their ornamented tree. The television in the corner reflects a funhouse mirror version of events as their silhouettes distort grotesquely in the dark screen. Jingle Bells plays quietly in the background.

"Time to open your last present, babe." Robert picks up a poorly wrapped item.

The paper concealing the gift is covered in pictures of Santa's visage. Based on the shape, Alice can't help assuming the item is a roll of cookie dough. She hopes Robert wouldn't save that for last. His grin seems far too large for him to be giving her such a mundane present. His excitement infects her as she tears Santa's face in two to reveal a plastic tube.

Alice comes to a slow realization. "Wait. Are these?" She pops the lid open and pours the contents on the floor.

Small, circular disks with pictures on them roll in every direction on the hardwood floor.

Tears flood Alice's eyes. "You got me POGs!"

"Do you like them?"

"Do I like this perfectly distilled package of childhood nostalgia? Of course." Alice collects the cardboard disks and stacks them back together. "I can't believe you remembered how much I wanted these. I hadn't talked about them in years."

"I listen sometimes. They're to replace the ones you lost when your house burned down in 95. Fun fact I learned while looking into these, POG stands for Passionfruit, Orange, and Guava because the game originates from kids playing with bottle caps for a drink with those juices mixed together."

"We both know you're a nerd, you don't need to reinforce it." Alice shuffles through the collection, surveying the different types. "Alright, looks like we got some X-Men to start: Cyclops, Rogue, and Archangel. Very cool. A Bart Simpson, of course. Not sure what these are, but I think they're from a Sega game. The Haunted Mask from *Goosebumps*, cool, several Power Rangers, many different Pokémon, which is ironic considering that craze basically killed the one for POGs, and the last one has a weird yellow scribble on it." She inspects the one with the yellow scrawl closest of all. Several lines swirl and intersect with each other at odd angles suggesting the appearance of a design, but there's nothing recognizable that can be definitively identified. While the other cardboard disks are clearly official POGs, this last one is slightly too small and heavy to be a legitimate POG. As she stares at the script, she can't help thinking she's about to discover a hidden word in the nonsensical symbol. Alice thinks it must be a lenticular image, but there is no evidence of lenticular material. "Where did you even get these?"

"Online. The seller sent them to me as a gift. He said he was in the Christmas spirit, and he didn't think anyone would actually shell out twenty dollars plus shipping for an old tube of POGs." Robert picks up one of the POGs and flips it like a coin off his thumb. "I kind of thought he was pulling a scam on me, but all he asked for was my address. The package showed up a week ago with no issues."

"These are rad." Alice tucks the disk with the yellow mark into her front pajama pocket and sets the rest down.

"Rad? Who still says that? Might as well let out a cowabunga or ask me to eat your shorts." Robert laughs as he leans forward. The rise in good cheer has caused a rise in other areas. "I love you."

Alice holds up a hand to stop his advance. "I love you too. That's why I'm not going to break off our engagement after you got me POGs instead of the super chic necklace I pointed out a month ago."

They both freeze in an uncomfortable silence staring at each other. Alice is the first to break as she starts to laugh, destroying her faux seriousness. Robert moves forward with lecherous hands finding the quickest way past Alice's holiday pajamas.

When they've finished their carnal embrace, Robert lays naked on the floor, panting and smiling with unrestrained glee.

Alice rolls onto her stomach and pulls her discarded pants closer. She removes the disc with the yellow marking from the pocket and rubs it between her fingers. The texture feels good against her skin, her cheeks flush, and she finds herself ready for another round with Robert, but this time she leaves the disc where she can see it.

2

On New Year's Day, Alice sits at the small kitchen table within her apartment. She sips mint tea to wash away the lingering taste of alcohol from the night before. Her favorite disc lies on the table, and she can't help staring at the yellow symbol adorning it.

Robert enters the kitchen, heading to grab a coffee mug. "Geez, you really like that present, don't you?"

"There's something about this writing." Alice sets her tea down and picks up the disc to examine it closer.

"Doesn't look like writing to me, just a faint yellow smear." Robert sits next to her with his freshly poured java.

"I think it's a letter from an unknown language."

"Uh, yeah. I'm sure someone making disposable cardboard disks for a 90s kids fad started printing a new alphabet on them."

"This isn't an actual POG. It's something else. Couldn't find anything online, but I'm sure the yellow lines signify something."

Robert stands up and grabs the disc. "It does feel different. There's more weight. But regardless, I'm starting to get concerned. You've had this thing with you since Christmas. Don't think I didn't notice you staring at it during sex this entire week."

"It's nothing to feel threatened by." Alice tries to go back to sipping tea but can't stop looking at the disc in her fiancé's hand.

"I just want to make sure I'm not missing something here. Could this be the start of another episode?"

"Relax. I can quit this thing whenever I want." Alice snatches the disc back and walks it over to the garbage can. She opens the lid and dangles the item above the accumulated waste.

"Point taken. Don't devalue my Christmas present by putting it in the trash."

Alice pockets the disc in her robe and returns to the table for tea. "Then don't overthink my interest. There's something soothing about it."

Robert finishes his coffee in a gulp. "I'll drop it for now." He leaves the room, and the sound of the shower running fills the apartment a moment later.

Alice pulls the disc back out and stares at it for a second before returning to the trash. She lifts the lid again and drops the present inside before heading to the living room for a morning workout. When Alice tosses her robe onto the couch, the disc rolls out of her pocket. She picks it up, stares at the yellow lines, and returns it to her robe.

3

"So, you think Punxsutawney Phil will see his shadow tomorrow?" Robert slides into bed.

Alice shoves the disc covered in yellow script beneath her pillow. "What does it matter? It's not as if it really determines anything."

"Blasphemy. You know that Phil is gifted with seasonal sight." Robert stares at her with his mouth agape.

Alice reaches out and shuts his lower jaw. "If Phil were blessed with weather divination, Staten Island wouldn't have created its own groundhog for forecasting."

"Staten Island Chuck is nothing but a no-good usurper. New York couldn't stop at having the greatest city in the United States. It had to steal Pennsylvania's groundhog tradition too. Outrageous. A scandal, I say."

Alice rolls away from Robert and prepares to drift off to sleep. She slides one hand under her pillow to grasp her disc. Robert cuddles up behind her. The heat of his body makes her immediately uncomfortable.

"Are we going to talk about what's in bed with us?" Robert asks.

"How about I don't judge your love of groundhogs named Phil, and you don't judge my need to sleep with this thing under my head." Alice pushes out her butt to tell Robert to scram.

Robert rolls onto his back and stares up at the ceiling. "Just seems weird, is all. I don't think I've seen you without that thing since you got it. Have you considered talking to someone? Besides me, I mean."

"Oh, I know exactly what you mean. I've had my fill of shrinks. Can we please just go to bed?"

There's no answer from Robert, but he rolls over to face away from her. It isn't long before she hears him snoring. Alice considers going to the couch because she can't stop thinking about Robert's infuriating suggestion. Finally, she manages to drift off to sleep despite her frustration.

She awakens soon after, except her bed has grown cold and hard. Alice sits up to locate her blanket, only to discover her small, one-bedroom apartment is nowhere to be found. Instead, she finds her mattress replaced with a black stone altar poking out of a rocky beach. Oily water laps at the shore as wind whistles around her. Twin suns cast a marvelous glow as they set along the horizon. Turning around, Alice spots a ruined city of crumbling towers and rubble in the distance.

"There's no need for fear." The message echoes through her brain, but she hears no voice on the air.

Alice scrambles off her resting spot in the unknown location. When her foot hits the rocky beach, she screams in pain and fear. Blood spills on the stones as she confirms she's sliced her skin open.

"You are in the presence of our splendorous capital. Take heart, not flight." The voice is cold and alien.

"Dream. Must be a dream. My dream. I'm in control." Taking deep breaths, Alice regains her composure. "That capital didn't look very splendorous to me."

"Look again."

She turns and witnesses the twin suns' last rays cascading over the dilapidated structures. Each one transforms as it's contacted. After a blink, the locale has changed into a golden city of spires and domes.

"Your parents and brother are waiting for you there. They can live again if the city is saved from the winter it has fallen into. The capital only needs more subjects to restore its glory."

"Leave it to my subconscious to reopen my deepest wounds." Alice leans against the altar and lifts her foot up to examine it. The cut isn't nearly as deep as she'd suspected. The blood trickles out. "Mentioning my family is a low blow, Mr. Dream-man."

"I am no dream. Gaze upon my form."

It sounds like a kid is blowing air down a straw, and then Alice looks up to see bubbles rising from the depths of the inky water. A yellow-robed form ascends just off the shore, an arm's length away. In the fading light, she can't make out the person inside, but she's impressed the dark fluid isn't clinging to the fabric.

"Clothing that can't get stained. Now this dream is speaking my language." Alice steps forward, causing rocks to clatter off other rocks and plop into the liquid's edge.

"Come no closer. Our time is nearly at its end. I'm here to deliver a message."

"Okay, subconscious. What do you need to tell me?"

"Spread the gift we gave you so that our world will bloom again. Our King needs subjects."

Alice disobeys the ban on approaching and takes three steps nearer, ignoring the pain in her foot. She reaches out to grab the robe. As she clutches it, a giant, wiggling worm retreats from out of the yellow fabric into the black liquid with a plop. A scream echoes out of her mouth and across the water.

She shoots up from her bed.

Robert stirs next to her. "Nightmare?"

Alice feels her pulse racing and sweat covers her forehead. She takes a deep breath. "Yeah. Nightmare. I haven't had one so real since I was a kid. Since after the fire."

"Well, it's over now. Back to sleep." Robert is snoring a moment later.

She lays back down, but the dream remains in her thoughts. *Spread the gift we gave you.* Alice reaches under her pillow and pulls out the disc. *Our King needs subjects.* As her adrenaline wears off, she feels pain shooting up from her foot. Alice knows what she'll find as she walks into the bathroom to check her injury.

4

The next morning, Phil sees his shadow. Robert delivers the news when he returns from the living room. Alice sits in bed, turning the disc over in her hand. Her eyes are bloodshot from lack of sleep.

"Robert, I know this will sound weird, but will you take back the disc you gave me? Just take it and give it away to someone or throw it out at the first chance you get."

"Sure." He buttons up his dress shirt as he readies for work. "I'm happy you've decided to move on from this thing." Robert holds out his hand.

She offers it over to him, but she's not sure if it will leave her hand. Alice can't help remembering the time she tried to throw it out. To her relief, it falls onto Robert's palm. He puts it in his breast pocket, kisses her goodbye, and collects his bag on the way out.

When Alice hears the door close, she gets out of bed to prepare for her own day of work. She heads into the bathroom and checks the scrape from the night before. It's healing as well as can be expected. Alice turns on the shower and lets the warm water wash away her worries.

5

As of President's Day, Robert has been missing for two weeks. Alice has spent the time since he failed to return home meeting with police, scanning social media for clues about his whereabouts, and calling friends and family. It all amounts to nothing. Robert left for work on Groundhog's Day and vanished before he got to his car. The apartment building recorded him in the elevator and walking through the lobby, but the parking lot cameras didn't get a glimpse of anyone going near his car that day.

Alice lies in bed with tears oozing down her cheeks. She can't handle how strange it feels to be here without Robert. She used to hate having to share the mattress, and now she can't rest with so much of it empty. Alice fixates on the disc she gave her fiancé while the nightstand clock ticks the hours away. Eventually, exhaustion forces her to sleep.

"Wake up, my dear."

Alice barely stirs as she answers. "Come back to bed, Robert."

Robert calls back. "You must awaken. I have so much to show you."

Wind whips the blankets from the bed. Alice is startled from her groggy state. She sits up to find herself in an unfamiliar setting. Her apartment has been replaced by a stone room with a large, open window and a wooden door. Carved into the exit is the symbol from the disc she passed to her lost lover. She shivers in the night air. Outside, the first rays of twin suns peek over the horizon.

"We can live together in eternal bliss as the King's subjects." Robert's voice comes from beyond the door. Heavy, plodding footsteps approach the room's entrance. "I can't wait for you to see how much I've changed. My extra limbs will bring you newfound ecstasy."

"I don't want to see you with extra limbs. Please, stay away." Alice hops off the bed and runs to the window. Golden domes and spires stretch off into the distance. Lightning arcs between the steeples as the domes swell and shrink like breathing organisms. She can just make out a large body of water beyond the structures. "I'm back in the dream city."

"This is no dream." Robert's voice is closer.

Alice climbs onto the stone windowsill. The height between her room and the closest dome is dizzying, but the ground is obscured in black clouds of sooty smoke. She inches back from the ledge as a bolt of lightning flashes by. Robert's steps are getting nearer, and Alice dreads seeing him. She runs to her bed. The heavy wooden frame doesn't slide easily, but once it starts to move, she gets it across the room in a burst to barricade the entrance.

A fist pounds on the door. "Open up."

"No. I can't see you. This isn't right. This place is wrong."

"How dare you? Our King needs subjects. Who are you to deny him? Who are you to deny me? I'm your future husband. Your future King. You must do as I command."

Alice can't stop the tears from leaking down her face. She's never heard Robert like this. The door shudders as he hits it again.

"Go away." Alice runs back to the windowsill. "A dream. This has to be another dream. If I kill myself, I'll wake up at home." She stares down into the black smoke below.

"Jumping is suicide," Robert yells.

"Don't come in, and I won't have to jump. I thought you loved me. Why are you doing this?"

The pounding intensifies. The door begins to give way with a crack as the wood splinters in multiple places. Light from the hall projects a monstrous shadow against the interior stones. Robert's silhouette has slithering appendages protruding from his shoulders, and his cranium is elongated into a bulbous, octopus-like shape.

She looks away as the wood creaks from more impacts. He'll breach the room in moments. Her heart beats like it's trying to spring from her chest. Alice can't look at the thing Robert's become. She follows her heart's example and leaps from the window.

Falling is pure freedom, and the speed of descent gives her a rush of euphoria as she approaches the smoke below. Another flash of lightning illuminates the world, and she spots yellow eyes watching her fall from an opening in the nearest dome. The smoke swallows her.

She lands on a soft, moist ground covered in snow. She shivers in the winter air. Hands pull her up, and Alice faces her deceased mother. The blue of her parent's eyes shines through the hazy surroundings.

"Mom?"

"I'm here, honey." She embraces Alice in a warm hug.

"Don't forget about us." Her father steps out of the dark clouds with her brother at his side.

None of them have aged since the fire consumed their flesh. No burn marks mar their skin. They all wear yellow robes like the dream-man in the lake, except their hoods are down.

"It's true? You do live here?"

Her father joins the embrace. His beard tickles her neck. "Of course."

"But only when the city has other subjects." Her brother adds as he hugs her waist. "You'll spread the gift and make the city bloom, right? You won't let us go away again? I'm tired of living here during winter."

His voice is so cute, it's almost sickening. Alice untangles herself from her deceased family. She surveys them for any sign of falsehood. Her brother is frozen at nine, in perfect boyhood. They seem to notice the disbelief washing over her face.

"Oh, honey, don't worry." Her mother approaches. "We've forgiven you."

"It wasn't my fault. The window was left open. The nor'easter blew the cardboard over."

Her father smiles as he opens his hands for another hug. "But it was your cardboard. You were so obsessed with that disc fad you were trying to make your own. You'd cut dozens of perfect circles out, and they fell onto the stove, caught fire, and rolled away. Who'd have thought one might find its way to the living room. I know I was surprised when the Christmas tree burst into flames while I was helping your brother put the star on top. But as your mother said, we've forgiven you."

Robert steps out of the black smoke surrounding them. "If you won't spread the gift for those you lost in the fire, do it for me, my love." He's garbed in the same yellow robe as the others, and his features are back to normal.

Alice tries to speak. "You were—"

"Overeager. You weren't ready for the new me yet, but once this city has more subjects, you'll see how wonderful it all is." Robert leans in for a kiss.

She returns his affections without a thought. "Don't let me wake up."

Robert gently pushes her away. "Sorry, honey. You've got to go back. You must spread the gift for our King." Her fiancé turns to face her formerly deceased loved ones.

Alice follows Robert's gaze to her family, who stand grouped together. They step aside to reveal another yellow-robed figure approaching. A snow-white mask without a mouth opening covers the person's face. The eye holes are too dark to make out anything underneath, but Alice knows who this is. The King reaches into his robe and reveals the disc she'd given to Robert.

The city begins to shake, and Alice looks down to see the ground undulating. The snow shakes free as a large white worm writhes to life under her feet. When she looks back up, everyone is gone. Only their clothes remain in piles beneath wiggling white tendrils, which retreat into the moving creature she stands on. A great maw opens below, and Alice falls into a mouth filled with icicle-like teeth.

She awakens in her apartment, covered in sweat. Freed from the dream, Alice tosses back her heavy comforter. A dozen discs with the yellow symbol lie on Robert's side of the bed. As she reaches for one, she realizes she is covered in soot and snow. Alice picks up a disc and feels relief flood into her. She's missed its weight, its texture, and its comfort.

For the first time since Robert's disappearance, Alice isn't worried about him. She knows he's waiting for her in the other world, the golden city that's fallen into winter. After a moment, she leaves her bed to gather envelopes and stamps. Alice brings up her phone's contact list, complete with physical addresses, and starts to work.

The Threshold

Part 1: The Doorway

Doug returned from work, removed his shoes, set his keys on their hook, and entered his living room to find a free-standing door where his coffee table should've been.

He surveyed the room carefully, looking for any other differences. His lumpy couch remained against the back wall with his *Game of Thrones* pillows tucked into opposite sides. His entertainment system resided opposite the large piece of furniture. The darkened television reflected the couch. Behind the door, he saw his kitchen. Nothing looked out of place.

"Josh? Is this some kind of weird joke? I don't get it," said Doug, aloud to his apartment.

He lived alone, but his best friend Josh was good at pulling off stunts like this. In college, Josh had successfully wrapped their toilet in plastic. Then he'd taken Doug out drinking. When they got home, Doug had to pee so bad he thought his bladder would burst. He didn't notice the plastic until it was too late.

Doug circled the doorway. The back side was the same as the front, a single hinged door in a frame. The wood looked like cheap plywood that someone had covered in a sea green paint. A single silver doorknob stuck out of the left side on both the front and the back.

A smile crossed Doug's face. "It can't even be opened."

He reached out and grasped the handle on the side facing his front door. To his surprise, he was able to push the door open. His stomach felt queasy like he was about to plunge down the steep tracks of a roller coaster drop.

"Josh, if you're hiding somewhere around here, you really outdid yourself."

Doug stepped over the threshold, closing the door behind him. He proceeded to the bathroom attached to his kitchen. The queasy feeling in his stomach remained. The coffee he'd had close to the end of his shift at work left his body, and he watched it cascade into the bowl. He flushed and began to wash up. As he scrubbed his hands in the sink, he stared at his face in the mirror above. Something about his reflection was wrong.

His goatee remained unchanged. He'd shaved it to make himself resemble one of those evil doppelgangers in *Star Trek*. The single freckle on his cheek looked the same. His hair still parted down the middle, splitting it into two, nearly even sections. But something in his mind still told him his reflection was wrong. The queasy feeling in his stomach grew worse when he looked directly into his own eyes. The bluish-green iris's he'd been born with twenty-four years ago were gone. Two black pupils stared back   at   him.
A loud pounding came from the front door.

Doug turned away from his reflection in confusion. When he looked back, the black pupils had grown larger; they'd nearly expelled any trace of white in his eyeball.

"Josh, how the fuck did you do this?!"

His stomach now roiled with discomfort and nervous tension. It told him what he didn't want to express verbally. Josh wasn't responsible for whatever was happening.

The pounding on the door came again. And again. It intensified to rapid strikes. Someone wanted to break the door down.

Doug returned to the living room. The closed-door remained where his coffee table had been. He could see his front entrance shaking with the continued impacts from whoever stood outside. Next to the entry, he saw the street through his living room window. His jaw dropped open.

Instead of a clear blue sky and a suburban street, he saw glowing crimson clouds blocking out a black ocean of night. The cloud light was so intense it made the decrepit structures outside cast shadows across the street. And as the clouds moved, the light caught whoever, whatever, attacked his door. Its shadow loomed large, with multiple twitching feelers.

He slapped his own face to shock himself awake. Doug knew he must be dreaming. This was a nightmare. The worst he'd had since childhood. A hinge flew off his front door and landed by his feet. The aroma of old fish wafted in through the spot where the entrance was being forced open.

Doug dashed forward, grabbed the handle of the free-standing door in his living room, and re-crossed the threshold.

Part 2: Destruction

Doug reached the other side of the threshold. Normal sunlight glared through his front windows and welcomed him back to the world he knew. Outside, the decrepit structures and crimson clouds he'd seen after first crossing through the doorway were gone. The street looked like the same one he'd glimpsed every day since moving in. He took great gulps of air in quick succession as relief flooded his body. A sudden crash shattered his composure.

His eyes darted to his front door to look for the thing that'd been trying to break it down when he'd crossed the threshold into the other world. The entrance remained standing, and the wood displayed no signs of distress. A slopping sound wormed its way through the room. Doug could practically feel the noise like a physical presence approaching him. Adrenaline coursed through his veins as his body navigated between fighting something he couldn't see or fleeing. With his senses heightened to their peak, he was able to better identify where the horrid sound came from. Behind him.

He turned to look through the open free-standing doorway. Inside, red light cast a grotesque shadow across his living room floor. The shape consisted of hundreds of spindly appendages squirming in different directions and reaching out from a huge singular mass. Doug looked up from the floor to see a piece of the worm-like arms slithering into view. With it came a smell like rotting fish. The thing was trying to cross the threshold.

Doug broke free from his frightened paralysis. He slammed the door shut. The noise and smell of the creature's approach ceased immediately.

Sweat poured down his forehead as he took in quick breaths. Doug feared moving to see past the thin wooden door. He trembled at the thought of glimpsing the thing's shadow still splayed across his living room floor.

The doorbell rang.

Doug turned to look at his front door. Someone was peeking inside his window. The radiant sunlight caused him a moment of blindness. His eyes adjusted, and the clear blue sky behind the figure came into view, followed by the person's facial features.

It was his best friend, Josh. He dressed in a casual hoodie and jeans. Stubble covered his jaw. He must've recently gotten a buzz cut. Doug shook his head in relief and walked to the front door to let his pal in.

"Where the hell have you been, man?" Josh asked, stepping inside.

"Ah," Doug struggled to find his words.

Josh walked into the living room. "What the—"

He'd seen the threshold. Doug stood behind him. The two stared at the free-standing doorway in silence for a moment.

"Odd decorating decision," Josh said, taking a seat on the couch. "Hey, the *Resident Evil 2* remake has been out for three weeks, and we haven't started our podcast about it yet. We've got a hungry audience of twenty-five people who've been harassing me about it on social media."

Doug ignored his friend and rushed to the bathroom off his kitchen. Inside, he turned on the light. The eyes that stared back at him were their normal blue-green color.

"Thank God," he said, aloud.

"Dude? You even listening to me?" Josh yelled from the living room.

Ignoring his friend, Doug exited his apartment via the backdoor in the kitchen. Outside, the brisk air sent a shiver through his body. He made his way to the fence and hopped over it into his neighbors' yard. An ax with a yellow fiberglass handle stood embedded in a block of wood. Doug wedged it out and returned to his apartment. He grasped the ax with both hands and raised it over his head. When he saw the doorway, he charged forward.

The ax went straight through the sea-green door's cheap wood.

"What the fuck?" Josh shouted.

Doug saw his friend's mouth hanging open. He leaned over to look past the door, to the spot Josh stared at. The ax Doug held wasn't sticking out of the backside of the door. He still gripped the end of the ax handle, but the rest of it wasn't visible.

Doug pulled the ax back. The sharpened head reappeared in their reality. He swung the weapon again, but instead of hearing wood splinter he heard the sickening squish of flesh being punctured.

"Stop," Josh cried. "Tell me what the hell's going on."

He ignored his pal's protestations and sent another strike at the door. Then another, and another. A sticky red substance oozed out from the damaged areas. It started to coat the ax. Out of the corner of his eye, Doug saw Josh scrambling toward the front door of the apartment. Doug kept chopping, and when he swung at the frame, the sound of breaking bone echoed in the room. He didn't stop until all that remained of the threshold were splinters of wood, or what looked like wood, lying in a crimson stain on his carpet.

"Had to destroy the door. Couldn't let that thing get out. No idea why it sounded like I was chopping up a living thing instead of a door," Doug said, through exhausted breaths.

He looked up to see that Josh had left the room. Doug didn't know when he'd gone, but he'd worry about it later. Now he needed to clean up the remnants in his apartment.

Part 3: Insanity's Grasp

The remains of the door in his living room were nearly gone. Once he dropped the ax back at his neighbors, he could start blocking this day from his memory. Doug prepared to toss the final pine scented garbage bag into the dumpster when red and blue light flashed across the alley.

"Drop the ax, kid," commanded an officer.

"I was just returning it." Doug looked behind him.

A cruiser idled in the mouth of the backstreet. One cop stood on either side of the vehicle. The words Arkham Police Department were spelled out in midnight gloss across the open door's snow-white paint. He'd never heard of Arkham before. The cop on the driver's side had one hand hovering over his pistol and one going for the bulb mounted by the rearview mirror. His counterpart leaned against the vehicle.

"That may be, but we'd like you to drop it all the same," the tilting officer said.

Light blinded Doug, and he raised his hand to block it out. He heard both officers react as their shoes clacked off the asphalt. His vision remained severely impaired by the luminosity.

"Easy Rookie. You're blinding the man," the same officer said. "And put your gun away for god's sake."

"But look at the bag," the other officer said. "It's leaking blood, and it's on the weapon."

Looking down, Doug saw the crimson substance that oozed out of the threshold dripping from a hole in the stretched plastic.

"Just sap," Doug lied.

"Listen, sir, you need to cooperate and drop the damn ax before we discuss anything else," the first officer who'd spoken said.

He complied, and the tool clanged against the ground when he dropped it. The main light beam elevated from his face to cascade across the alley above. The driver-side officer who'd negated the blinding bulb raised his pistol to aim at Doug.

The leaning officer straightened his stance. "Now, why don't you try explaining this all to us, nice and slowly."

***

Four hours later, Doug sat in a windowless room in white scrubs and sandals. He focused on the small table in front of him. There was a brown stain he couldn't stop staring at. The shape reminded him of a door.

Footsteps approached from down the hall, and the door creaked open. Officer Hodges re-entered the room with a small, well-dressed man behind him. They made a truly odd couple as Hodges's white dress shirt was crinkled and stained by his lunch, while a pistol hung in a holster under his armpit, and the other man looked like he'd ironed his entire suit before dawning it.

"Mr. Williams, this is Doctor Bierce. He's going to be handling your stay tonight," Officer Hodges said. "And your neighbor decided not to press charges since the ax was undamaged, so they'll be no further involvement from us." Officer

Hodges went to the door before turning back for a moment. "I hope you get the help you need here." He left.

Doctor Bierce shut the door and approached with his hand out in greeting. "How are you feeling tonight?"

"Honestly, I'm a bit pissed at my friend Josh for calling the cops on me." Doug slouched forward in his chair. "But maybe it's for the best that he did. I mean, what the hell did I tell the cops when they found me? That I'd found a door to another dimension in my living room and a monster tried to eat me?" Doug chuckled quietly before starting to laugh louder.

Doctor Bierce sat across from him. "Laughter is good Mr. Williams. Laughter is healing."

Doug kept laughing. He started pounding the table enthusiastically. His sides started to hurt, and tears started to flood his eyes. His jovial mood sank into sadness as he began to sob. Doug didn't know why.

"What you truly need is a good night of sleep." Doctor Bierce removed a two pack of pills from his upper jacket pocket. "Follow me to the nurse's station, and we'll get you some water to wash those down with. Then we have a nice bed waiting for you upstairs."

Doug wiped away the tears and followed the doctor out of the room into the hallway. "Did they ever figure out what the red stuff on the wood was?"

"Conclusively determined not to be blood, but I did not hear exactly what it was," Doctor Bierce said. "Here you are.

Nurse Barnes will handle things from here. We'll talk in the morning."

Nurse Barnes looked younger than Doug. In another situation, he might've even tried to strike up a conversation with her. Her fiery red hair was pulled back in a ponytail.

She slid a paper cup of water toward him and grabbed a clipboard. "Best drink up before I take you to your room."

Doug cracked open the plastic holding his pills and downed them with the liquid as a chaser. Nurse Barnes gestured for him to follow, and she led him to a nearby staircase. They proceeded to the second floor where the sound of a low moan started.

"What's that?" Doug asked.

"A Deep One."

"What? What's that?"

"Really, Mr. Williams. You need your rest." Nurse Barnes stopped in front of an open door with her arm held out toward it.

Doug hesitated. "You won't be locking me in, right?"

Nurse Barnes smiled, her ruby lipstick and hair shined in the overhead light. "We don't do that here."

He entered the room. It was bare. The walls and floors were padded, and a solitary bed and toilet stood opposite each other with a barred window between. Doug noticed a huge brown stain on his blanket. It instantly reminded him of the one on the table downstairs. He turned to tell Nurse Barnes he needed a replacement just as she shut the door. The click of the lock echoed in the hall outside.

"Wait!" Doug rushed to the door. "You said you wouldn't lock me in."

He peered through a small, barred opening in the door. Nurse Barnes ignored his protestation and walked away from him, returning the way she came. Doug pushed on the door, but it was firmly shut against him. He rammed it with his shoulder and instantly regretted the action as pain shot down his side. Looking into the hall, he spotted a cell across from his. The patient inside stared at him.

"You're not from our reality," the patient said. "You've crossed a threshold. Allow me to be the first to welcome you to the dark side of the world."

Part 4: Tasty, Tasty Treat

The setting sun sent searing rays into his eyes. Doug didn't know how long he'd been locked in the asylum. He spent so much time sleeping that he sometimes missed the sun's rise and fall. The days and nights swam together like mud and shit. *Must be at least a week*, he thought. *Maybe two?*

"Won't be long now," the inmate across the hall said. "I'm ascending tonight."

Doug cuddled closer to the wall to avoid the blinding light. "That's great Howard. I'm really happy for you."

He wasn't. Doug didn't feel much of anything anymore. Talking to Howard was all he had to do, but every interaction made Doug feel less connected to reality.

On the first night, Doug screamed and railed against his confinement. By the middle of the next day, he'd decided his only way out was to play nice. No nurses ever came to evaluate him though, and the orderly who shoved food through the small slot at the bottom of the door, once a day, wore headphones to avoid conversation. It wasn't long before he decided to start responding to Howard's daily assertions and inquiries. It was all he could do besides eat, sleep, and use the toilet.

First, Howard explained how the asylum wasn't actually an asylum. Doug pressed him on what it really was, but the inmate wouldn't elaborate. Next, Howard went into a long technical rant involving dark energy, black mass, and the atomic inverse formula, Doug comprehended almost none of it, but the thrust of the confined man's ramblings seemed to argue that they'd both crossed into a dark inversion of the world they'd been born into. The skin of their planet had been sliced open, turned inside out, and stitched back together to form this one. Doug had almost believed that the man was once a physicist, as he claimed, but that night Doug watched Howard drink his urine and rip out his hair for a snack.

"No questions about the ascension? That's not like you. You were so inquisitive when we first met."

"Howard, I just want to sleep until they let me out of here." Doug stared at the thousands of tiny tally-marks the previous occupant had made. "If they ever let me out of here."

"But you'll get to see it for the first time tonight. It's beautiful and stark, but the wrapping is just a façade. Don't forget that."

Doug chuckled. "I won't."

Sleep throttled his waking mind.

***

Clack, Clack. Clack, Clack. *Steps. Someone's finally coming.* Moonlight now illuminated his cell. Doug scrambled out of bed so fast he fell to the floor, surprising a rat who dashed into the darkness under his cot. At least one rodent snuck into his room through the food slot every night. He got up to peer out of the barred window in his door.

The fluorescent lights reflecting off the tile floors dimmed and went out. Doug's eyes tried to adjust. Clack, Clack. Clack, Clack. The steps continued to approach in the blackness. A sound, like a dog whose tail's just been trampled, penetrated his ears from a faraway cell.

"Howard, what's happening? Is this the ascension?"

The lights burst back into life and died again before adopting a continuous flicker. Down the hall, a living void of midnight walked toward Howard's cell. After a disbelieving blink, the form looked familiar, human. The man wore jeans, sneakers, and a grey pullover with the hood covering his face.

Clack, Clack. Doug focused on the man's footwear. The sound didn't make sense with the rubber soles. The clacks sounded like they belonged to a woman in high heels. The bizarre dissonance unnerved him more than the imagined shape he'd seen. His stomach tightened, and a voice in the back of his mind told him to hide, to climb under his bed and cower with the rat, but this was the first person he'd seen without headphones since the nurse had left him here. He needed to try to get his attention.

Doug gently knocked on his door. "Excuse me, would you have a moment to talk?"

The approaching figure stopped in his tracks two doors down from where Howard and Doug's cells stared across the hall at each other.

"What the hell are you doing?" Howard hammered on his door. "I'm ascending tonight. I've been here for months. You're not ruining this for me."

Clack, Clack. The hooded figure took two steps forward. Clack, Clack. The man took two more steps. His idiosyncratic walking made Doug wonder if he was an escaped patient.

Now that the man stood closer, Doug noticed that no hands resided at the end of either sweatshirt sleeve. Clack, Clack. He stood between Howard and Doug's rooms and raised an arm to each side.

A hot flow of air, like a dog's breath, caressed his face through the bars. A deep sniff came from inside the hoodie's sleeve. Doug's heart pumped faster as he fought against the urge to dive under his bed.

"Oh," the man in the hall said. "You both smell of other worlds." The voice sounded like it came from far down the hall.

Howard slammed his head against the bars. "You want me. I've been here longer."

The hood turned toward Howard. "Yes, but you've lost a good deal of the other world's fragrance. It's an aphrodisiac you know. Tonight will ensure I sire new children within the next eon. Why wouldn't I want more of that?" The hood turned toward Doug.

He stood frozen in the eyeless gaze of the stranger outside the cell. The man wore a white mask with only a smile and a nose carved into the ivory-like material. Doug backed away from the door. He couldn't look away, but it was all he wanted to do. He hit the wall before he realized, and the white mask began to bubble and drip as it lost its solidity. A wiggling piece of gray flesh emerged from the man's sleeve, and it split apart into several tendrils as it stretched past the bars of his door.

Behind the thing, Howard hocked up a phlegmy wad and spat it at the hood. It stained the sweatshirt, and where the saliva darkened the cloth smoked. All the lights reached a sudden crescendo of luminosity and burst. Freed from the horror of sight, Doug dove under his bed. He felt the rat's fur against his forehead.

The animal had lost control of its bowels nearby. In the fetal position, he closed his eyes tightly as the metal of his door was rent asunder with a horrible twisting screech.

"Tasty, tasty treat, why do you hide?"

Part 5: Escape

Pain drove Doug out of unconsciousness. His first thought was a bug bite, but when he opened his eyes, he saw a rat attempting to make a snack of his right nostril. The rodent dashed over his face before his hand connected with it. Blood trickled from the small wound onto the rotten linoleum floor. Doug tried to sit up and smacked his forehead on the frame of his bed. His mind struggled to recall how he'd ended up here.

Moments from the night before flashed through his mind, but he couldn't concentrate on any. It felt like they'd been sent through a paper shredder. Without knowing why, a lesson from undergraduate psychology class floated into his thoughts. *The mind forgets to protect itself.* Doug slid back out from his hiding place and found his room destroyed.

Instead of a toilet at the back of the cell, there now stood the remains of his door. The solid metal was compressed on the outer edges. It looked like a giant had squeezed it several times. The bars were all ripped out and lay twisted and scattered across the floor. One had pierced his pillow. The image of a grey hooded man approaching down the hall shot into his mind's eye. He nearly screamed in terror, but he didn't know why.

Doug ignored the thought and turned to confirm that the entrance remained unbarricaded. The way was open, and the position of the sun outside the barred window indicated he'd have a good amount of time before the headphone wearing orderly delivered his sustenance for the day. Escape was suddenly possible.

Proceeding to the door, he leaned out slowly to confirm the hallway was empty. It was. Silence filled the asylum as dawn trickled rays of light throughout. Doug stepped outside, and he noticed that Howard's cell was also missing its door.

"Howard?" Doug whispered. "You in there?"

He stepped closer and heard a squeak. Then another as he took another step. Dark red liquid entered his vision as he leaned his head over the threshold. The realization of what he looked at took a long moment. He followed the trail of blood as it curved around the linoleum floor like a river viewed from space. When he finally reached its end, he wished he'd not checked on his former cellmate.

The corpse that used to be Howard was covered with fur. Doug's eyes adjusted to the dim light of the cell. The fur seemed to move, and then Doug made out small, beady eyes, teeth, and claws amongst the throng of brown hair. Rats swarmed over Howard's body, ripping flesh away in small bites. One squeaked at another as they fought over Howard's index finger. Doug wanted to look away, but as he did, his gaze landed on Howard's head. The man's eyes were gone, and Doug felt himself start to feel truly sick, but when a rat climbed out of the empty skull, he spewed the minuscule amount of food he'd been able to eat since being imprisoned.

"Stay right there!"

Doug looked up to see an orderly who'd just entered the hallway from the far end. It was the man who brought him food, holding three stacked trays of disgusting hospital fair, but he hadn't put his headphones on yet. Doug didn't have time to think, so he let instinct take over and charged forward. The orderly dropped the food and attempted to flee back to the door he'd entered from. The man pulled out a set of keys and slid one into the door lock. Doug collided into him with all the strength he could muster. The orderly's head slammed off the steel bars. The crack reverberated throughout the room. Doug let the man fall to the ground with his keys. It was only as he lay unconscious on the ground that Doug noticed how young he seemed. Probably no older than twenty.

"I'm sorry." Doug kneeled to pick up the keys. "In a normal–" Doug struggled to avoid laughing at the absurdity of the unfinished statement. "Normal. What the hell does that mean anymore? Listen, kid, I hope you're okay, but I can't take another day in here."

He picked up the keys and tried each one until the door opened. Just beyond the threshold, he spotted an empty guard station. Inside, a hooded jacket hung on a rack. Doug hoped it would be enough to disguise him on the way out. He stepped out of the hall and shut the door behind him. Doug locked it, for good measure.

A walkie talkie broadcast a static message from inside the room. "Have you fed the livestock yet Carpenter?"

Doug entered the guard station and dawned the coat. He zipped it up to cover the top of the white scrubs he'd been asked to change into upon his arrival. The small slip-on-sandals would be a dead giveaway, but he hadn't thought the orderly's small sneakers would fit his feet.

"Dammit, Carpenter, I hate staying here a second longer than necessary. Feed those lunatics and get back to the car."

He surveyed the room for the walkie talkie and found it sitting next to the surveillance computer. The small communications device looked brand new, but the PC next to it looked ancient. A thick layer of dust coated it. Everything in the room, but the jacket and the walkie, seemed outdated. Doug grabbed the device and turned the volume down before heading away from the guard room.

The closest door opened to reveal a staircase. Doug descended and paused at the first large window. Outside, an old fence surrounded the grounds, but the forest had encroached on it severely. Several sections were rusted or bent over. The state of the place was horrendous. He hadn't noticed when he'd arrived in the dark. Doug continued down and used the keys to gain access to another long hallway. He didn't spot anyone residing in any of the adjoining cells. Each was empty, and the furniture inside was ancient, rusted, and dusty.

"Carpenter?" The voice from the walkie echoed down the hall.

Doug ducked into the closest room. He dashed behind the door but ensured it didn't shut. Footsteps grew closer. Whoever the other man was picked up his pace and started running.

"Come on, dude. I hate this spooky ass place. Answer your god damn walkie."

The steps passed and started to grow fainter. Doug waited until he heard the door to the stairs open and shut before he crept out of his hiding spot. The mystery man had left the exit wide open. Fresh air rushed in from outside. The sound of chirping birds greeted Doug's ears, and best of all, he heard a running motor. Doug sprinted to cross the asylum's threshold and escape.

Part 6: Extraterrestrial

The car sat idling outside Doug's sister's apartment. He hadn't seen her for a long time now. He'd thought about going over to Josh's, but his time in the asylum hadn't cooled his rage toward his friend. He never would have been tossed into that horror show if Josh hadn't called the cops on him. *Some friend.*

Doug turned the car off and took a deep breath. Without heat from the vehicle's engine, the fall chill made its way into his bones. He picked up the phone, which the car's owner had left in the cupholder, and brought up the map again. It didn't make any sense to Doug. He didn't recognize the name of the city he resided in, but he knew many of the streets and roads once he got a short way from the asylum. He decided it was a question for his sister. She was the smartest person he knew. She'd gotten a master's degree.

He checked to make sure no one was looking before darting out of the car toward her front door. Doug hit the buzzer and waited. His breath came out in quick smoke-like puffs. Every sound made his head dart in the direction of the noise. He didn't how long it would be before the cops, the nurses, or whoever owned the car found him.

"It's about time," his sister said while opening the door. "I ordered that pizza nearly an hour ag—"

Doug waved stupidly. "Hey, Ellen."

Her freckled brow crinkled into a scowl. "Where the hell have you been?"

"Inside?"

She stepped aside, and he entered her place. It was just as Doug remembered it. Geeky paraphernalia adorned every surface. A Lego Captain Marvel guarded her key hook, a Pop Vinyl Doctor Who stared at him from a bookshelf, and a stack of books and comics, mostly *Saga*, littered her entryway. Doug proceeded into her living room and collapsed into his grandma's old couch. She'd inherited it instead of him, and they'd argued about it for years.

Ellen shut the door and followed Doug into her residence. "So, what's the deal?"

"I don't have the slightest fucking clue. I might be losing my mind."

"You never had a mind. Why are you wearing contacts?"

"Huh?"

"Your eyes. Why are they that weird shade of ocean?"

He sat up straight. "I was born with these eyes."

"No. You were born with brown eyes. Like me." She gestured to her irises behind her trendy silver glasses.

Looking where she directed, Doug saw her eyes really were brown. Every memory of their eyes ran through his head and confirmed that they'd both grown up with the same bluish-green eyes. Their parents both had them too.

"I need to tell you about the past few days."

***

The pizza arrived halfway through Doug's recitation of his journey to her door. He started with the threshold in his living room, touched on his encounter with the asylum entity only briefly, and concluded with his flight to her home. He left out all the most demented details, the rats eating his hall mate and his own attack of the orderly. Doug hoped he hadn't killed the man, but the unease in his stomach, due to the cracking sound the man had made when he fell, hadn't gone away.

Ellen finished her second slice of pineapple and red-pepper pizza. "So, you claim you're from a town called Hazel Peak that has some streets in common with our city?"

"I'd never heard of Arkham until I found it on the GPS."
A memory flashed through his mind. "I mean. I sort of remember thinking it was odd that the police who picked me up had the word written across their cars, but I just assumed they weren't local cops."

"Well, I guess you were born dumb in that other reality too."

"What do you mean?"

She stood up to point at the TARDIS model hanging from her ceiling. "You've traveled to another dimension like the Tenth Doctor. When you came back through the threshold, you didn't return to your original reality, you ended up in another new one. I mean, that is if I choose to believe you haven't just gone insane."

Doug smiled, but his already upset stomach roiled in discomfort. The three slices of cheap pizza hadn't helped anything. Now he just felt gassy and ready to fall asleep.

"In your dimension, you and I had different color eyes, and our town was called Hazel Peak instead of Arkham. There are probably a zillion other differences you'd notice if you had a more analytical mind."

"Did you just insult me again? After the time I've had?"

She darted over to her collection of movies and television shows. "It's kind of like *Sliders*, the 90s show. Why did you get to go on the super cool dimension-hopping adventure? The only science fiction you like is *Extraterrestrial*."

"What the hell is *Extraterrestrial*?"

"You know. The movie Ridley Scott made with Sigourney Weaver?"

Doug raised his hands in confusion. "*Alien*? With the Facehuggers?"

"Hmm. Seems like we found another weird difference in our universes. Honestly, if I'd been the one to go on this adventure, it would've made a lot more sense."

"Adventure? I've been nearly killed by horrible things multiple times now. Not to mention being locked in an asylum."

She tossed Doug her copy of *Sliders* on DVD. "As I said, adventure. This is so cool."

He didn't remember his sister being so friendly and excited around him. The two had barely talked in the last four years. Their dad had kept them in contact, but once he'd died, they'd drifted apart. Growing up, they hadn't been all that close to begin with.

"Is Dad still alive here?"

Ellen's enthusiasm vanished. "No. He died about four years ago."

Doug set the DVD down on her coffee table. "Damn. I guess nothing is better here. Just different."

"Well, we've spent a ton more time together since then. We even started our geek review podcast. Although you let Josh jump in about a month ago. Well, I mean, I guess that wasn't you. Which raises the question. Where is the Doug from my dimension?"

He shook his head to show her how little he understood his own situation. "Maybe he's in my world? Better for him since we don't have monsters."

She blew a stray hair away from her face. "I've never seen monsters here, but Arkham's a city of strange folklore and witch legends. My time reading through the rare books at Miskatonic hinted at a lot."

"I've never heard of that university. What state are we in now?"

"Massachusetts."

Doug threw himself back into the couch's comfort in an exasperated fit. "Hazel Peak was in Pennsylvania. I've traveled to another dimension and another state."

"Yeah, traveling to another state sure is freaky." Joked Ellen. "Maybe something about the rotation of the earth causes the portal to spit you out in another region of the country?"

Violent knocks shook them out of their conversation.

He stood up and grabbed the replica Arwen sword that hung next to the couch to defend himself. "Whoever owns that car found me. Or the police. I won't go back to that asylum!"

Ellen turned to him with a smile. "Don't worry brother from another world. I've got a plan."

Part 7: Back to School

Doug followed his sister out her back window. He'd left the sword behind to avoid unnecessary attention, and he'd managed to find a pair of her sneakers that just barley fit him. They circumvented the apartment complex to determine who knocked at her front door. They both peaked around a nearby wall to spy on his sister's front stoop. A tall, blonde man in a long grey coat, jeans, and a checkered dress shirt stood waiting for someone to answer.

Ellen whispered. "Do you know him?"

Doug whispered back. "No idea. He might be the other guy from the asylum."

"We should just conf—"

The man withdrew a pistol from inside his coat.

Ellen motioned for Doug to follow and took off jogging in the other direction. She led him to her nearby car, a blue hatchback with *Dr. Who* stickers covering every inch of the bumper. Doug got in and turned back as Ellen accelerated away. The blonde man raced to the edge of the street and raised his gun at them. His sister turned the car off the block, and the man vanished behind suburban houses.

Doug took in panicked breaths. "That guy was going to shoot at us."

"Just chill. He should have no way of knowing where we're going." Ellen focused on the road as they merged onto the highway toward downtown Arkham. "He probably had some kind of tracker in his car, and we're not using it now."

***

The campus of Miskatonic University came into view as they ascended college hill a little past sundown. Doug noticed the ornate marble façade of the Orne Library before any other buildings. It practically shined in the darkness. Ellen parked the car in the visitor lot next to a large concrete dormitory. It didn't fit in at all with the rest of the campus, which looked somewhat reminiscent of Brown University. He'd visited Brown with his sister from his own reality when she was choosing where to go for higher education.

Doug turned to his sister. "What are we doing here?"

"My girlfriend is staying in the dorms while she attends a conference." Ellen opened her car door.

"What does that have to do with my problem?"

"She's smart, and she knows all about higher level dimensional gateways."

"What?"

"Just wait here." Ellen got out of the car and headed for the door.

Doug let his head slide down into his hands. He felt so tired after the day of frantic travel, the reconnection with his sister, and three slices of pizza. When he looked up, his sister had vanished from view. He put his seat back and closed his eyes.

***

A crack of shattering glass jolted Doug back to waking life. A blood moon shined down on the car, and he felt the spray of cool wind across his face. Adrenaline pumped into his system as the blonde man with the gun came into focus just a few feet away, outside the smashed driver's side window of his sister's car. Doug tried to dart out his side, but the seatbelt halted his attempt. He frantically went for the button to free himself, and a deafening blast rang through the car. The shot destroyed the buckle and blood gushed from his hand.

The blonde man leaned into the window. "Don't move. You're food for the Living Void."

Doug froze up in fear. He now knew how deer felt when they saw oncoming cars. There was nothing he could do.

The man reached in and opened the door from the inside while keeping his gun pointed at Doug. There was an odd popping sound, and the blonde man started shaking. His face contorted into an expression of rage, and he collapsed onto the seat next to Doug. Two small wires trailed out of the blonde man's butt to a security guard behind him.

Doug felt his body freed from paralysis, and he dashed out of the car to scramble into a heap on the university common.

The security guard walked over to Doug. "You okay?"

Doug looked down at his hand and saw the blood trickling out slower than at first glance. The bullet had just grazed the tip of his ring finger. Relief flooded into his body. He looked up at the security guard, who wore a gray uniform and a little badge displaying his name, Juan Ramirez.

"I think so."

"Cops are on their way."

Two women approached the scene, and Doug turned to confirm one was his sister.

Ellen ran toward him. "What did you do to my car?" She noticed the passed-out man and stopped. "Damn."

Doug got back to his feet. "The guy from your apartment found me."

The new girl joined the gathering. She had frizzy hair sprawling out in all directions and an assortment of necklaces with different symbols at their ends, stars, moons, leaves, crosses, and keys. "Professor Ward, extra-dimensional mathematics and occult studies, primarily." She offered her hand.

Doug shook it in a daze. Cop lights appeared in the distance, and the sirens brought students filing out of the nearby dormitory to investigate. Ramirez kept his eyes glued to the incapacitated man.

Ellen whispered something to Ward, and then she turned to Doug. "We don't want to be here when the cops arrive. Your sister filled me in on your situation. I believe I can help, but we need to move quickly."

Part 8: Miskatonic Tunnels

Doug followed his sister and Ward as they rushed across the campus quad toward the Orne Library. The building's grandeur belonged to an ornate time in America's architectural history that had long since vanished, at least in his reality. Inside,

138

Ward paused to exchange words with a receptionist at the front desk. Doug surveyed the endless rows of books spanning multiple levels. Some students browsed, while others hunkered over open books scrutinizing the pages.

"Your pass gets you access, but I'll have to check with Dr. Sanders before I let your guests through," said the receptionist, a well-dressed work-study student with an expensive-looking blazer.

Ward smiled. "That's fine. We'll wait here while you check."

The receptionist left the desk, and as soon as he was out of sight, Ward gestured for them to follow her. She pulled a badge from her pocket and flashed it past an electronic lock, which beeped. The group filed through the doorway down a flight of stairs into a dimly lit tunnel.

Ward acted as a tour guide as they hurried forward. "There are miles of these passages. Some are filled with books, and some are filled with objects. One of the alcoves holds a freestanding doorway that only appears when the stars are in a very specific alignment."

"How come you never told me about these before?" asked Ellen.

"I was sworn to secrecy, babe. Besides, how believable would my story have been without the proof of your dimensionally displaced brother here?"

Doug felt pain pulsing up from his bullet-grazed finger as he tried to maintain the pace of his female companions.

Ward continued the tour as they made a right turn into a new corridor. "Of course, the professors here have studied the doorway to death, but no one ever felt brave enough to cross the threshold."

"Well, I wasn't brave, I just assumed my friend had played a weird practical joke on me. Nothing looked odd on the other side of the doorway." Doug replied.

"Nothing looks odd on the other side of this one either, but the door gives off harmless levels of radiation, mild heat, and occasional rays of light." Ward led them around another turn into a long recess where they came face to face with the topic of discussion.

This freestanding doorway didn't look as cheaply made as the one Doug had encountered in his apartment. Instead of a wood frame, it had coal-colored stones outlining a frosted glass door tinted a deep yellow. A short distance set it apart from the brick wall behind it, and the air felt much warmer around the object.

Ellen immediately reached out to grasp the door's handle, but Doug snatched her arm back. "Careful. You don't want to end up like me."

"Adventuring across dimensions? That's exactly what I want. You think it's fun to live an ordinary, dull existence working for a corporate giant while my arts degree rots in a frame on my wall?" Tears formed at the edge of Ellen's eyes.

Doug tightened his grip on his sister's arm. "You can't be serious. I told you about all the horrors I've seen since the door popped up in my life. It's been a nightmare. You're the only good thing I've found so far."

Ward pushed the siblings apart. "We don't have time for this. Listen."

A clatter of footsteps reverberated off the stone floor behind them.

Ward turned to Doug. "I don't know if this doorway will lead you back to your world, but this is probably the only chance you'll have to try. The stars will be out of alignment in a day, and they won't be back in position for eighty years. You have to choose between the unknown and staying here with us."

A yell flew down the hall toward them. "Stop. This area is restricted."

Doug looked to his sister, a family member he'd grown distant from in his world. Arkham wasn't the city he knew, but it was better than the other reality he'd glimpsed when he first crossed the threshold into the orange sky world inhabited by a tentacled beast. This version of earth was different, but he could make a home here. Yet, he didn't know if he could fully commit to saying goodbye to everyone he'd ever known or loved back in his reality.

Someone flew past him, and a sickening crunch snapped Doug out of his deliberation. The receptionist lay against the wall with his head crushed in. Doug averted his gaze from the horrible sight.

"What is that?" Ward yelled.

Doug spun to stare back the way they'd come. Memories of the asylum rushed back to him in a painful flood. Clack, Clack. Clack, Clack. The lights in the hall started blinking furiously, struggling to work. A man wearing jeans, sneakers, and a grey pullover with the hood covering his face approached from the other end of the hallway. In an instant, Doug knew this thing from the asylum was what the man who'd tried to kill him called the Living Void.

It called to the group in a quiet voice as it approached. "Tasty, tasty treat. I just couldn't stay satisfied with my last meal. You were so much fresher; I could smell you from the asylum."

Ward and Ellen were frozen in fear. Doug knew he couldn't leave them here for the thing to kill. "We're trapped. You both have to come with me."

The Living Void's voice cracked the walls. "You're my aphrodisiac. You smell of other worlds. You can't leave. My children will be born of your flesh."

Ellen and Ward broke from their terror trance and turned toward the door. In that instant, the Living Void flashed out of existence. The lights returned to normal.

Doug let out a sigh of relief. "He's gone. I don't know why, but he left."

"Very unlikely that it's actually gone," Ward said.

"It's our chance. Let's get the hell out of here." Ellen started running back the way they'd come before Ward or Doug could stop her.

Blood flew everywhere as Doug's sister exploded in a million directions. The Living Void reappeared in the space she'd died with a crimson coating. The lights resumed their flickering.

Ward let out a scream of despair. Doug felt his center vanish. He'd only really known the Ellen of this reality for a day, but she'd been a better, closer sister then he'd ever had back home. Now she was a pile of pulp through which a monster padded. Numbness flowed into his body, and he felt relieved to flee his emotions.

It was all too much. His nerves were overwhelmed and burnt out in the surge of grief.

The Living Void reached out its handless arms for Ward. It would grasp her and do something just as horrible to his sister's lover, and then it would eat Doug. In a flash of adrenaline-fueled madness, Doug grabbed Ward's shirt collar and yanked her backward as he spun to pull them both over the threshold of the freestanding glass door.

The being behind them let out a cry of childish agony as they emerged into warm yellow sunlight. Doug pushed Ward behind him as he turned back to slam the door before the Living

Void could reach it. His force shattered the glass into trillions of tiny shards. The hallway of Miskatonic University's lower levels vanished as a castle wall appeared in its place. A single window displayed the sky outside, where twin suns were setting.

"She's dead. She's dead. She's dead." Ward had collapsed onto the stone floor. "She's dead. She's dead. She's dead."

Doug's numbness made surveying their new surroundings seem pointless. He sunk next to Ward and pulled her into a hug of mutual despair as the tears came to both of their eyes in rivers. They sat together until the lights vanished, and it wasn't until the suns rose again that either of them talked or moved.

"The doorway might still be open. The physical representation is destroyed, but the link between worlds could still exist." Ward whispered.

Approaching footfalls reached their ears a moment later. In the light, they saw that the coal-like threshold stood in the middle of a stone room. Doug's first impression was that they'd wound up in a castle, and the morning confirmed that assumption. The only entrance to the room, aside from the dimensional gate they'd used, was a wooden door with a brass ring in the center. The door opened.

A woman garbed in a faded yellow robe entered. "Welcome to Carcosa. My name is Cassilda. Our King would like an audience."

Part 9: In the Court of the King in Yellow

Doug and Ward followed Cassilda down a spiral staircase. He'd been unable to get a good look at the woman's visage. It remained obscured behind her yellow hood. Their guide glided down the smooth steps with no difficulty, but Doug struggled to avoid slipping. A steady stream of black water cascaded along one side of the stairs, making the entire surface slick. He kept using the wall to stabilize himself. The few windows they passed revealed a landscape covered in dark clouds. He thought he could just make out a golden spire in the distance of one window, but he wasn't entirely sure.

Another twist of the tower brought Doug around to face a missing section of the wall. Wind whipped in through the opening, and inky raindrops stung his face. Behind him, Doug heard the squeak of Ward's lost footing. He turned to stop her slide before she sent them both to their deaths, but she collided with him before he could get his feet set and they both tumbled out of the hole.

Doug scrambled to grab onto anything as he fell, but his fingers slid off wet stones.

They landed with a splash. Doug swam to the surface and looked up at the breach in the tower. They'd only fallen a few feet into an overflowing fountain. A decrepit statue jutted up from the middle. He had no idea what the eroded golden nub had once represented. His companion surfaced next to him.

Ward spat out a mouthful of water. "I hope this king has dry clothes."

"Me too." Doug swam to the fountain's edge and pulled himself out and onto paved cobblestones. "Where'd our guide go?"

"She's right there." Ward clambered out to sit next to him.

Cassilda stood at the entrance to the tower, awaiting them. Doug surveyed the city they found themselves inside. Unlike the previous world he'd visited, this one didn't look remotely like his own. There were no suburban houses, modern skyscrapers, or old colonial universities. Instead, he saw towers and domes of gold. Their architectural styles weren't familiar and some of the tall structures seemed far too thin for anyone to fit inside. The domes had a wave-like quality to their structure that reminded him of lava formations he'd seen on the Discovery Channel. A tremendous crash of thunder and lightning drew his gaze to the sky.

The rain stopped abruptly, and the black clouds shifted to a dull orange. After a moment, they swirled into a vortex that revealed a purple sky above. Twin suns blazed overhead. Doug felt his moist skin and clothes begin to dry as soon as the heat of the stars reached him.

"I don't think this is another version of Earth." Ward stood up and held out a hand.

Doug used the assistance to get to his feet. "You can say that again."

Cassilda walked past them. "This is Carcosa."

Doug and Ward looked at each other for a moment before they followed her again. As she'd passed, he got his first good look at their guide's face. She wore a mask displaying female features, snow-white skin, emerald eyes, ink-drawn black eyebrows and lips. The dimness of the castle and the storm had hidden it well, but in the light of the two suns, the mask was shown to be a mere imitation of humanity. Her faded yellow robes now glittered as veins of silk were illuminated.

They walked through alleys and tunnels, twisting and zagging through the streets of Carcosa. If there were any inhabitants in the city besides the trio, they did not make themselves known. The silence was only broken by their footsteps and the occasional crash of thunder in the distance.

His mind drifted back to his sister's last moments in Miskatonic. She'd been exploded from the inside out. He couldn't stop seeing her blood dripping down the Living Void's body. His brain played the moment on a loop. While he felt gutted over the loss, every time he looked at Ward, he felt greater sorrow. While he'd known an Ellen his entire life, he'd only known the Ellen of that world for a day. Ward had been her lover. Now she was stuck here with him and the knowledge that the last thing she saw in her own world was her girlfriend being murdered.

"Wait here." Cassilda stopped before two enormous doors, they seemed to be carved out of sapphire.

Their guide continued walking, circumventing the entrance. Doug and Ward stood in place before a domed structure that had several spires sticking out of the top. Lightning struck the tallest and an arc of electricity shot between the others. Orange clouds swirled in from the distance and formed a column through which he could momentarily see a night sky filled with stars.

Ward remarked on the phenomenon without amazement. "This place is obviously some kind of spatial and temporal nexus. Nothing seems to be consistent here. It's amazing anyone manages to live in this world."

The sapphire doors swung open to reveal yellow stairs leading up to a darkened room filled with ancient, petrified trees. Doug grabbed Ward's hand for his own comfort. They ascended together and followed an amber carpet to a sandy beach. A great lake stretched to the edge of the horizon, and he looked around to confirm they were still inside the dome. The structure opened to form a gigantic space. For a moment, Doug thought they'd come into a normal-looking area of Carcosa, but a closer inspection revealed that the blue sky and white clouds were colored walls. He saw a few areas where the paint had peeled to reveal grimy stone underneath. Out of the water in front of them, a form rose.

Doug took a step back, but Ward remained in place. They were still joined at the hand. The figure wore a yellow robe, like Cassilda's, but a crown of thorns sat upon the head, and the mask covering the face was white and featureless aside from the mouth and eye slits. The robes billowed loosely, and the sleeves hung without arms inside. Doug was reminded of the sheet ghosts that people put on poles for Halloween.

Cassilda walked up behind them. "You are in the presence of the greatest entity of Carcosa. The Un-nameable. Bow in reverence."

Doug and Ward acted as instructed.

Cassilda moved to stand between them and the being in the water. "The Un-nameable does not degrade himself with conversing, and he usually doesn't deign to traffic with lower forms, but this is a special moment for Carcosa."

Ward leaned close to Doug and whispered. "Of course, this thing still thinks of itself as a man and has a woman to do his work."

"You have traveled to this world without a summoning, and you've performed no ritual to arrive. This makes you trespassers, but in your foolishness, you've led in an offering for the Un-nameable." Cassilda gestured behind them.

They both turned.

The Living Void approached. The being that had been trying to eat Doug for days walked quickly over the yellow carpet and through the long-dead forest. The creature threw off its grey pullover and stepped out of its jeans as it progressed. The articles of clothing were still soaked in his sister's blood. Without the disguise, the Living Void's form became that of a night's sky in human outline.

"You were right, the gate between worlds wasn't closed when the glass door shattered. It followed us." Doug wrenched

Ward to the right so they could try to avoid being sandwiched by the two entities.

Cassilda gestured to the sand behind her, and two stone seats rose. "Due to the magnitude of this food, which you've directed right to us, you will be given the honor of watching the un-nameable feast. Your mind will be rendered useless, but no lower form has ever been gifted such grace."

Doug spotted the outline of a door against the far wall, behind the two stones, and started pulling Ward toward it. The sight of their follower had frozen her feet to the ground.

The shadowy form of the Living Void continued toward them without regarding the two figures in yellow. "Tasty, tasty treats. Don't run any further. I've already pursued you here. Let me get my fill. I want the children you will allow me to spawn. Be my aphrodisiac."

A tremendous wave of water exploded out of the lake and drenched Ward and Doug. Their recently dried clothes were soaked again. Out of the tumultuous churn rose the yellow-crowned king. Instead of two legs, the un-nameable had a massive white tentacle puppeteering his robes. The appendage led to a huge gelatinous body. More tentacles slithered out of the form's central mass toward the Living Void. A tremor ran through Doug's body. Blood trickled from his nose. A primal part of his nervous system, something left from when his ancestors ran from lions in the jungle, told him that looking any longer would mean death.

Doug turned away and charged toward the door on the far wall, dragging Ward through wet sand. Cassilda glided around to block their escape. She stretched out her arms like a scarecrow. Behind him, he heard a titanic struggle as water splashed and old trees splintered apart.

"If you don't move, I'm going to punch that stupid mask right off your damn face," Doug shouted.

Cassilda retorted, "But I wear no mask."

Ward leaped forward, suddenly coming to her senses, and made good on Doug's threat. Her fist penetrated Cassilda's face, and the robes collapsed in on themselves, revealing nothing inside. Doug followed Ward to the door. They pushed it open together, and a grassy hill topped with a stone archway was revealed. Through the archway, Doug saw a shimmering vision of his apartment building.

"That might be my home, and even if it isn't, it will be better than here. Come on." He shouted over the chaotic sounds of battle behind them.

Doug and Ward dashed up the hill.

Part 10: The End?

The dimension dodging duo dove over the threshold, leaving Carcosa behind. Doug and Ward landed in a heap on the sidewalk outside Doug's apartment. Whatever rip in time and space led them to that spot was no longer visible.

"We made it," Doug said.

Ward dusted herself off and got to her feet. "But, where are we?"

"This looks like my place, but so did your world." Doug stood up and surveyed the area.

His apartment was a ground floor in a three-story building with tenants above and across from him. The street was a well-manicured block with small homes of different shapes and sizes stretching in either direction. It was wholly unremarkable, which is what made the appearance of approaching military vehicles entirely remarkable.

Doug looked for a direction to flee, but he saw military camouflage everywhere. His muscles were all drained from their hasty exit from the King in Yellow's lair. He couldn't help wondering who'd won the titanic clash between the Living Void and the Un-nameable. Doug hoped the Living Void had gotten his just desserts.

Ward grabbed his hand tightly, and they shared a look of resignation. Their friendship was new, but it was bonded in the fierce trials they'd faced. Now, whatever would be would be.

An olive-green jeep slammed on its breaks, and soldiers popped out with weapons raised toward Doug and Ward. "On the ground, now."

They did as they were told. More soldiers piled out of the arriving trucks and vans. They looked ready for war.

One of the troops crept nearer with what looked like a Gameboy. "Anomaly is clear, Ma'am."

A white-haired woman in the starred uniform of a general walked forward. "Thank God. If Hastur had made it through, we wouldn't have stood a chance." Her cold blue eyes fell to Doug and Ward. "Tranquilize these two until we come to a consensus on what to do with them."

Doug popped up to argue, but a dart pierced his neck before he managed a single word. The world blackened. His body fell back to the pavement.

***

When his eyes opened, Doug found, to his horror, that he'd been re-confined to a cell. Thoughts of the Living Void coming for him flashed through his head. Thoughts of his sister being killed followed. His heartbeat increased, and he took a deep breath to try and calm his nerves.

This cell was much nicer than the last one he'd been put inside. Everything was newly cleaned, and his sheets felt soft and fresh. Outside, he could see a green field stretching to a busy road. Civilization was within reach. His cell door opened with a clang.

"Mr. Williams. Follow me, please." A soldier led him down the hall to a small room, where the general sat awaiting him.

The general gestured for Doug to join her at the room's lone table. "Come in. This won't take long."

Doug did as he was instructed. His body felt like it was on autopilot. He assessed his odds of escape if he bolted, but he was confident that he wouldn't make it off this floor.

"You've been through a lot. We're terribly sorry this happened to you. Our scientists should've identified the gate before it appeared in your apartment. It's a miracle you made it back here. Now, all you need to do is sign this paper, and you go back to living life." The general pushed a document forward. "It's a fairly standard non-disclosure agreement. You don't go telling the world that portals to other dimensions can occasionally pop up out of the blue, and we won't keep you imprisoned for the rest of your life. And we're providing you with a new apartment, and a small donation to make sure you reacclimatize to life here."

"Don't you even want to ask me what I experienced?"

"We've got all we needed from Ward. She's an extremely useful find for us."

"Where is she?"

"Classified."

"I won't sign unless I see her first."

"Fair is fair. Maybe you'll change your mind in a month or so." The general gestured to the soldier behind Doug, and he was grasped and pulled backward.

The idea of being tossed back in a cell broke him, and tears flooded out of his eyes. "Wait, I'll sign. Just don't put me back. Please."

***

Doug hesitated before he crossed the threshold into his new apartment. It had been six months since he signed the paper, but he still hadn't recovered from his ordeal. Thoughts of what he might find kept him from ever barging inside. Usually, he stood on the landing for a solid ten minutes. Doug took a deep breath and entered his home.

Inside, he found nothing out of place. Doug headed to his computer and started his nightly ritual. He searched the internet for any mentions of Ward. Doug visited tabloid news sites, crackpot YouTubers, and every other corner of the internet he could find discussing the topic of inter-dimensional doorways. As usual, he came up with nothing substantial. He logged off, readied for bed, and laid there, unable to drift off to sleep.

He found it hard to get rest because he had nightmares. He dreamed of Carcosa. The Living Void called to him from that bizarre city's highest towers. He asked if Doug would be his tasty treat.

Doug turned his mind to a different subject to avoid thinking about what he would see when he slept. He focused on his recent happy moments. He'd reunited with his sister, Ellen. Although she wasn't the same sister he bonded with so thoroughly in another dimension, Doug found that they hadn't grown as far apart as he'd believed in his own reality. They went to lunch every week, and he fought the urge to tell her all about his experiences. The thought that telling her the truth might put her in danger kept him restrained. Doug wasn't so blind as to miss his nearly constant government tail, but he's thankful to have avoided a cell. Even now, he's certain that if he got up and looked out the window, he'd see a black car idling on his block.

Doug left that frustrating subject and thought about his best friend, Josh. They'd recently restarted their podcast. Doug's mysterious disappearance managed to generate some new listeners, and they'd just run a contest to see who could come up with the best explanation for his having vanished for a week. None of the submissions came close to the truth.

With his good thought reserves drained, Doug found himself thinking about Ward again. As a woman from another dimension, he knew the government could do whatever it wanted with her and suffer no punishment. He contemplated the razor blade under his sink, but he knew his suicide wouldn't atone for signing the paper. It would just relieve him of his responsibility to her. Doug held onto a slim hope that Ward would manage to escape and make contact on her own. Until then, he planned to keep looking for any sign of her on the internet. He knew he didn't just owe Ward; he owed his sister from the other dimension for having led her girlfriend here.

Outside, the wind picked up in intensity as Doug fell away from consciousness.

In his dream, Doug wandered a zigzagging street through Carcosa. The sky had turned a bright red, and it looked like flames spread over the horizon. A spire crumbled to ruins next to him, and he watched a dome cave in to block his path. A night sky in human shape, the Living Void, emerged out of the rubble.

Doug tried to flee, but the ground turned to liquid, and he sunk to his waist.

The Living Void approached. "Tasty, tasty treat. I survived my encounter, and I'll soon find my way to you and your friend. Don't think you've escaped me. You'll still be my aphrodisiac. You, and everyone in your world."

The Sheriff and the Samurai

1 : Draw

Steam wafted into the sky from the approaching locomotive, which chugged to a stop along the recently completed transcontinental railway. I reached into my jacket and removed my pocket watch. 10:15 AM exactly. The small, wooden platform was deserted, except for me. This stop, if you could really call it that, had only been erected to serve the silver rush at Midnight Mountain, Nevada. The mountain was given the ominous moniker because a slightly taller peak kept it in the shade past noon. Of course, recent events had made the place more sinister by far. Unless I was mistaken, I assumed the papers in San Francisco were covered with headlines about the murdered Japanese diplomat during November 1869. That had been three months ago. And now, sooner than I'd like, his brother, who was supposedly some kind of warrior, was arriving to investigate.

The metal behemoth at the front of the train drifted past me, leading the bright red passenger cars into view. Although it was mid-winter, the day was hot as the sun hung high in the clear sky. I took off my Stetson hat and fanned the sweat from my face. My dark, black suit was the fanciest thing I owned, but it was a terrible choice on this warm day. The gold of my badge gleamed in the morning light. At last, the locomotive came to a full stop, and the door to the car in front of me slid open.

A slick, well-dressed government man with an oiled and curly mustache stepped out. "Sheriff Barron?"

"That'd be me." I returned the Stetson to my head.

"This one's your problem now. See that another of these savages doesn't end up dead in your care. You may've been someone in the war, but if I have to come back out to Nevada again, that won't stop me from making you wish you'd never been born." The government man headed back into the train.

My hand drifted down to the grip of my revolver. I considered shouting after him and challenging him to a duel. I was sure his pencil-thin arms couldn't even raise a gun, but then my new charge appeared.

The man before me was dressed in a fancy, grey robe, and he wore sandals instead of boots. His hair was done up in a knot. I would've mistaken him for a woman, if not for the two swords, one long and the other short, tucked into his belt of fabric.

"You Saigo?" I asked.

"Yes." His facial expression tightened in anger. "And you are the fool who allowed my brother to die."

I'd had enough insults for one day, and my grip tightened around my revolver's handle. "I didn't even know your brother was on Midnight Mountain until I found his corpse."

"Is it not your duty to protect those in your province?" Saigo's hand went to the longer of his two swords. "Do you think you could draw that gun before I cut off your arm?"

I weighed the challenge for a moment, seriously considering the implications of drawing.

The government man returned and tossed a bag past Saigo. "The train will be back tomorrow, and I expect the Japanese national on it."

Saigo and I both removed our hands from our weapons.

I picked up Saigo's bag, which was moderately heavy, and walked down the steps to the two horses I'd tied to the hitching post. "Hope you can ride. We're going up into the mountains. Should be to the camp by the afternoon."

"I can ride better than you can protect." To prove his point, Saigo dashed past me and vaulted up onto my horse.

Yet another insult. The day didn't seem to be getting any better. I hadn't experienced this kind of aggravation since I'd been caught behind enemy lines during General Sherman's March to the Sea. Thankfully, that situation hadn't lasted long, and I'd managed to fight my way back to my compatriots in blue.

I slung the bag over the back of the horse I'd brought for Saigo, my horse now, and I tied the bag up so it wouldn't fall. "What do you have in here?"

"Armor."

"Doesn't feel like metal. Who wears armor these days anyway? You a knight?" I mounted the horse I'd been left with and started off toward the mountains.

Saigo followed. "I am a Samurai, and the armor is light because it is not made from metal."

"Sam-ooo-rye." The word felt funny coming off my tongue. "You sure speak good English for a foreigner. I never could master any language but the one I grew up with."

"My people adapt fast. We've had to learn a great deal about your country since your Commodore Perry fired upon us." Saigo spurred his horse to go faster. "We're wasting time with idle talk."

The shrubs and sand of the desert surrounded us. Ahead, the flat land rose steadily to meet the mountains in the distance. I spurred my horse into a gallop to catch up with my new Japanese acquaintance.

***

Dark clouds blotted out the sun as we ascended the final slope into town, which was truly more of an overgrown mining camp. An accumulation of thirty wooden shacks thrown together by workers, a saloon, my dwelling, and the Company Store made up Silver Springs, a wishful name if there ever was one. The large, snow-topped peak that kept our settlement in the shade loomed above Midnight Mountain's nearby summit. No one came out to greet us. The men would still be in the mine at this hour.

I turned to my charge. "Where to first? You want to rest a while? Take in a drink, or maybe visit with one of the local women?" I smiled.

Saigo's facial expression remained grim. "Take me to where you found my brother."

"Straight to business it is." I directed my horse to the trail leading out of town.

The path was short and rocky. We didn't really need the horses to get to the mine, but I hadn't seen a point in dismounting to walk the span on foot. Silver Springs was only about eight wagon-lengths away when I brought my beast of burden to a halt. The hole carved into the mountainside was black as pitch. Wood was used to frame and support the tunnel's structure. Dismounting, I noticed how quiet it was. There were none of the usual sounds of pickaxes, falling rocks, or hard labor.

Saigo joined me on the ground, and we both hitched our horses to a nearby stump. Two unused lanterns sat outside the gaping maw of rock. Inspecting the lanterns, I found one broken, but the other looked fine. I removed my pack of matches from my pocket, sparked a flame, and lit the lantern in turn.

With my light source held high, I stepped over the carved-out threshold. "You have any idea why your brother was in this place?"

"His business is mine to know."

Thunder echoed outside, and a deluge started as we got undercover. I ducked to avoid the low, jagged roof, but Saigo fit with ease. We made our way down the rocky descent until the only light was from my lantern. Finally, we reached a junction. I turned left and led Saigo into a chamber bigger than any building we'd erected on the mountainside.

"Your brother was found in here." I continued forward.

162

"You were able to carve all this out?"

"No, the miners found this place. I assume it's a natural formation. There has been a lot of excitement in town about a passage they discovered leading off from here." I pointed to a large, smooth stone that jutted up from the earth. "A worker found your brother on this rock here."

"What else can you tell me about how he was found?"

"I suspect you may know more than I do about that since you know why he was here in the first place." I held the lantern up higher, and the light revealed a large bloodstain. "He was tied to this rock, and we found daggers piercing his shins, forearms, and one in his—" I paused. "You sure you want to hear all this?"

Saigo nodded.

"One dagger was in his groin. Don't ask me why." I took a breath and tried to recall what I'd missed. "A key shape had been carved into his cheek too."

I heard Saigo remove his sword from its sheath, and I spun around. The samurai brandished his blade toward the darkness behind us. I held my lantern out further. The light revealed a miner, whose eyes glowed like emeralds, holding a bloody pickaxe.

The man raised his weapon above his head, ready to lash out. "So happy you could join us here in the dark."

My hand went for my revolver, Saigo prepared to strike, and the miner lumbered forward.

2 : Aim

I drew my gun and pointed it squarely at the approaching miner's chest. From this range, I could probably put my bullet right between his glowing, green eyes, but I didn't want to risk missing my shot. Every second counts in a fight, and I didn't want to give my foe any extra time to send his pickaxe into my face.

Saigo took matters into his own hands before I could decide whether to fire. The worker's arms were severed in two cuts that whooshed through the air. There was a serene moment when the limbs slid apart like tree branches, and you could see the internal bone, tendons, and veins. After that, blood spurted everywhere as the man screamed in pain while his pickaxe clattered to the ground.

The miner's blood splashed over my face, and Saigo pivoted to aim his blade at me.

I cocked the hammer on my revolver. "Hold your horses. I don't know what's going on here. When I left this morning, we didn't have any miners with emerald peepers."

"Is this what you did to my brother? Led him into the mine, isolated him, and killed him?" Saigo raised his blade.

I fired.

My bullet caught another miner before he could complete his sneak attack on my Japanese associate.

"What say we discuss this once we're out of here?" Holding the lantern and gun in opposite hands, I rushed out of the cavernous chamber and back into the main tunnel.

Saigo followed. We moved quickly, but I worried the warrior might put his weapon through my back. I prayed that samurai were honorable.

The clatter of rocks and dragging metal alerted us that we were being pursued. How much of the workforce had gone mad? And what had triggered the change?

Someone grunted from behind us, exerting effort. There was panicked chirping. I turned back to see what was happening when Saigo collided with me. We tumbled to the ground, and my lantern shattered in a fiery heap near my hand. Saigo's sword just missed skewering me. A small, metal cage lay next to us with a dead bird inside. One of the miners must've thrown it.

Saigo pushed himself up and grabbed his sword. He turned to face the darkness. There were eight sickly, green eyes glowing an indeterminate distance away.

I regained my feet and used the destroyed lantern's fading light to aim and fire five shots past Saigo and toward our menacing pursuit. None of the bullets ricocheted off the surrounding rocks, and grunts of pain echoed around us. I'd hit at least one of the miners.

I pivoted around and ran. "Come on."

As the last of the flames died, Saigo tailed me.

After only a few more steps, we were in total darkness and needed to slow our frantic pace. The ominous sounds were quieted, but my heart pounded loudly. I splashed through a growing puddle, and the dull light of the rainy day appeared ahead. Water was flowing into the mine from the raging storm outside.

We exited the tunnel at a run, and I took a gulp of moist air. The expanse of open space was a relief after the oppressive rocky walls. I glanced behind us, but there didn't appear to be anyone following. My clothes were soaked as water spilled off my Stetson.

I unhitched my horse and mounted. "We need to see if anyone in Silver Springs can tell us what the hell is going on and get out of here if they can't."

"Coward. We should cleanse this place of the evil that grips it." Saigo stood at the mine entrance with his sword out.

The rain slowed, but the sun was starting its descent, putting the sky into a darker shade of evening. From inside the tunnel we'd left, there came a murderous cacophony. Dozens of men roared in anger.

Saigo sheathed his blade, unhitched his horse, and joined my side. "I will go with you to think further on the best course of attack, and I want to see my brother's body."

I didn't comment on his change of heart.

Together, we descended back to town. I kept twisting around in my saddle to make sure no one was pursuing us, and I used the ride to reload my revolver. When we got closer to the dwellings, no candlelight flickered anywhere despite the growing gloom. Thankfully, the rain had stopped completely.

I directed Saigo to the saloon, where I dismounted and left my horse. My spurs jangled loudly on the wooden floor as I entered the establishment. The four tables were overturned. There were bullet holes in the bar, and several of the chairs were smashed to splinters. Mercifully, a single bottle of whiskey remained pristine on the shelf behind the bar. I jogged over, hopped the barrier, uncapped the liquid, and took a swig.

Saigo appeared in the doorway. "My brother. I want to see him."

"What's the point? Don't you see what this place looks like? Whatever happened to those miners happened to this town when I was gone too. What the hell could've done that? A disease?" I took another swallow of whiskey. "No reason to stay here any longer. Silver Springs is a lost cause."

Saigo walked forward and snatched the whiskey from me. "No. What started here could spread. Do you value your country so little that you'd let this wound fester?" The samurai took a drink of the liquor and smashed the bottle on the bar.

Despite the loss of my liquid courage, Saigo's shaming inspired me to action.

"You're right. Follow me." I hopped over the bar again, left the saloon, and headed to my quarters.

Inside, there was a desk and a single jail cell. I grabbed a shovel and ventured to the back of the building. A small wooden cross marked where we'd laid Saigo's brother to rest. I started into the soggy earth.

Saigo kept watch as I did the work.

I didn't need to dig long before the shrouded corpse appeared, accompanied by the smell of rotting flesh.

I tossed the shovel and bent down to grab the body's shoulders. "You better be able to tell me something useful by looking at him."

Saigo grabbed his departed relatives' feet. Together, we hauled the waterlogged body out and carried it to my desk inside. I lit candles to give us additional light. Exhausted, I collapsed into my rickety wooden chair, opened a drawer, removed a handkerchief, and covered my nose to halt the malevolent odor's punishment.

My Japanese compatriot approached the body and pulled back the shroud. His brother's eyes were sunken pits, and the skin had turned a dark, ashy color. Saigo flipped open his brother's western suit jacket and felt around for something. When he located whatever he'd sought, he pulled hard, and the fabric ripped away to reveal a secret pocket. Inside, a piece of paper covered in Japanese characters was hidden.

I sat forward. "What's that say?"

Saigo pulled out the paper, unfolded it, and read it. "My brother was meeting a man here, in your mine."

"Who would want to meet in a mine?"

"His name was Howard King."

Recognition came at once. "He's the head of the Company Store here. Struck me as a bit stuck up. What did your brother want with him?"

Saigo stared at me like I was a piece of meat he wasn't sure he could stomach. "I'm going to trust you with a secret, Mr. Barron. I do this because I don't think we'll make it to tomorrow without aiding each other." Saigo walked to a nearby candle and burned the paper. "Japan isn't just committed to becoming a technological equal with the United States and Europe. We seek to reach the same level of adeptness in occult matters. What you might call magic. My brother's mission was to gather knowledge on the subject and return to my country."

"And Howard King was going to show your brother something about magic?"

"He claimed this place to be a powerful focal point for mystical energy. My brother's note talks about a dormant force in the mountain. King was going to show him how to access it."

I stood and covered the body back up with the shroud. "But what really happened was that King sacrificed your brother to unleash whatever has infected Silver Springs."

"That observation appears accurate. Is there a way we can seal the mine?"

"Yeah. We can dynamite it. Don't know how I'll explain my actions, but that should keep whatever's in that mine from getting out."

"I will get my armor. I suggest you load up as well. Together, we will halt whatever evil is growing beneath the mountain."

I took off my suit jacket, rolled up my sleeves, and withdrew my belt of ammo from the bottom drawer. Saigo headed outside and got the bag with his armor. He returned and lovingly removed the pieces and attached them to himself. Each section was a dark navy color, and he covered his chest, shoulders, thighs, shins, and forearms with protection. When his suit was completed, he dawned a helmet with a face shield that gave me the distinct impression of a demon's visage. The mouth slit was formed by vicious looking fangs, the eye holes were ringed by what looked like fire, and two horns curled from the forehead.

"The dynamite is in the Company Store around the corner." I headed toward the door and pushed it open.

Outside, the last traces of the storm clouds had drifted away to reveal a bright star-filled sky. A gibbous moon hung low in the sky, and a man stood a few feet away. He was well dressed in a grey suit with a black bowler hat. His beard grew to a point, and he smiled mischievously. Howard King had come to greet us.

3 : Fire and Cut

I drew my gun, cocked the hammer, and put Howard King's skull in my sights.

Saigo shouted through his demon mask. "Why did you kill my brother, you swine?"

King laughed. "It was all fun and games. Your brother was so eager to learn, and I needed a foreigner's blood. Well, he learned. He saw magic no human eyes have witnessed before, but he didn't count on enduring pain no human body had felt before as well."

"The miners. What's with them?" I asked.

"They're thralls to an ancient power now, but I got what I needed in exchange for leading them to its resting spot. I trust you'll be able to handle the situation. I've got other places to be." King stroked his pointed beard, and his face's skin melted away to reveal a black skull with quill-like fangs and four squirming tentacles where his lower jaw should have been.

My finger squeezed the trigger, and my target vanished like smoke.

I kept my gun raised and ready to fire again. "What in tarnation?"

"He's not a being like us," Saigo said. "Sadly, my brother's vengeance must wait for another day. Let's continue to the dynamite."

I returned the weight of my gun to my right hip and led my Japanese ally. As we walked, I squeezed my fist tightly to keep it from shaking. I'd seen horrible things before, but I'd never seen anything supernatural.

The Company Store was bigger than all the rest of the buildings in Silver Springs, but not by much. Inside, the few goods stocked were scattered on the floor, and most of the shelves were tipped and broken. A room in the back contained the dynamite, but an enormous lock held the door shut.

Saigo swiped it off.

I collected the closest crate of dynamite. "Now, we've got to be careful here. Just last week, I saw a miner split into several pieces when he mishandled this."

Saigo nodded. "You carry it, and I'll make sure no one gets close to you."

I considered arguing the point but decided that would only waste time. Who knew how long we had before the miners came swarming out to town? From the looks of things, something had turned the initial miners, and they'd come to collect the others in town. They could be back at any moment.

After carefully loading the crate and a new lantern onto a small wagon and attaching my horse, Saigo and I made our way up the mountainside by the light of the moon. We went at a snail's pace, but I still winced every time the wagon wheels went over anything larger than a pebble. The mine entrance came back into view, and two men with pickaxes and green eyes stood guard.

Saigo withdrew his sword and charged before we could discuss battle plans. The miners spotted him, and instead of moving to attack, they reached out for each other's hands. The two men's flesh seemed to liquify, and they fused into a hybrid thing with four legs, two arms, and two heads. They reminded me of a sideshow I'd seen on my way west years prior. The newborn thing scuttled forward, swinging the pickaxes wildly.

Saigo ducked and swung his sword, making it through three legs before his blade got stuck in the fourth. The conjoined miner wobbled and fell but managed to connect a blow to Saigo's chest. My Japanese ally's armor prevented penetration, but the samurai was hurtled backward and tumbled a few feet down the mountainside toward Silver Springs.

I brought the wagon to a stop and went to help Saigo regain his feet. As I got him up and dusted him off, he pointed behind me. I turned to see the mutated miner standing on his two arms while his remaining leg flailed about. Saigo's sword flew loose and clattered the ground. The thing's midsection split open to reveal an array of rib-like teeth that opened and closed as if the miner's maw had relocated. It charged us, and I pulled my gun and fired. My first two shots ricocheted off rocks, but then one of the scuttling arms exploded from my blast, and one of the thing's heads was pierced by my last bullets.

To my shock, my hits didn't slow the beast. I slid bullets from my belt to reload. The miner-monster slammed into me.

On the ground, I felt something bite into my foot, making it through my thick boots. Seconds later, I was being dragged, and I lost the bullets in my hand. My head scraped off a rock as my hat sailed away on the breeze. Everything went dark as the conjoined miner dragged me toward the mine.

***

I was shivering from the cold air when I returned to consciousness. I went for my revolver, only to realize it wasn't on my hip. A ring of six unarmed miners surrounded me on the stone dais where I'd found Saigo's brother. Their green eyes stared beyond me. A crimson light oozed out of the passage that led deeper into the mine. It had been the spot the mining company had been so excited to explore. To my relief, I wasn't tied down.

The group cried out at once. "To the Living Void, this flesh is offered."

I stood up and slid my legs off the stone. The miners weren't disturbed, so I got up. I approached the gap between two of the miners. They didn't react. Taking a breath, I dashed forward. The group spread out their limbs, which stretched and merged to fence me inside. They were now one massive, circular thing. I couldn't tell where any individuals ended because even their clothes had changed and morphed.

There was a loud gust of wind, and Saigo's blade cut through the limbs before me. The conjoined mass of humanity screamed. I rushed out of the circle.

Saigo turned and fled with me close behind. Just as I thought we'd be lost in the darkness, a dimly burning lantern appeared. Saigo sheathed his sword, grasped the lantern's handle, and didn't stop moving.

The sound of something large scraping off rocks followed us. I pictured the miners, changed into a giant burrowing worm.

Fresh air reached us, and we escaped the tunnel for a second time that night. Outside, I collected my lost gun from near the mine's mouth and reloaded quickly. Saigo brought the horse with the wagon forward, nearly to the mine entrance.

As I detached my horse, a glob of human flesh reached out of the mine. The individual miners' skin had stretched and distended in hideous ways to form the huge, wormy shape. I withdrew my gun and fired at the monster, sending my horse running just in time to escape the clutches of the thing.

Saigo grabbed my shoulder. "You fool. That thing's not going to be stopped by bullets."

I took Saigo's meaning and ran down the hill a short span before spinning back around. The mass of fused miners was pushing past the wagon filled with dynamite. I took aim, inhaled deeply, made sure I had my mark, and fired.

The explosion eviscerated the piece of the monster that had managed to escape and sent rock flying into the air. Saigo and I were sent sprawling from the blast.

***

Warmth kissed my cheek, and I thought of the time I'd spent a week in a New Orleans saloon with a woman named Rebecca. I opened my eyes, and I realized the first rays of the sun had woken me up. I'd spent the remainder of the night unconscious on the mountainside. My clothes were covered in an accumulation of rocks and dust. Blood smeared through some spots, but I didn't feel any screaming wounds. My current injuries were nowhere near as bad as the bullet I'd taken while riding with General Sherman.

My body ached from lying in the same position for hours, but I managed to get to my feet and dust myself off. I reclaimed my gun from where it lay and holstered it. The night's events flooded back to me, and I glanced up to the mine.

The dynamite had done its job. The entrance was sealed by rocks. Nothing could get in or out without more dynamite or more workers. The thought of whatever entity had forced those miners to go mad and combine bodies still lurking in the dark made my skin crawl. I could only hope that whatever force resided there wouldn't figure out how to burrow out. The clops of a horse approached and made me turn around.

Saigo rode up to me on what had once been my mount. "I apologize, but I must take my leave if I am to catch my train."

My ally had taken off his armor, re-bagged it, and cleaned up in the time I'd been left out in the cold.

"You could've woken me."

"I couldn't find you in the dark. I did try for a short time. The rocks must've concealed you."

I didn't buy the excuse, but I also didn't care to disagree.

"Then I guess this is the end of our partnership." I offered my hand for a shake.

Saigo stared at my hand for a moment, but he slowly offered his own.

I gripped his hand firmly and shook it once.

The hint of a smile crept across Saigo's face. "I'm sure my government would prefer that I killed you for sharing the secret of my brother's mission. If word reaches me that you've told anyone, I will return for your life."

Now it was my turn to smile. "Provided I ever let you close enough to hack at me with that sword again. Besides, you can tell your government and that pencil mustached bureaucrat you arrived with that I am dead. Things will be less complicated for me that way. Are you going to try and pursue Howard King?"

Saigo nodded. "Of course. I'm honor-bound to avenge my brother."

"I think I might look into his affairs myself. I owe him for what he did here. If I get word on him, another partnership might be in our interest. Is there a way I can reach you if I need to?"

"If all goes as planned, my people will be establishing an embassy in San Francisco soon. Get word there, and it will reach me eventually." Saigo turned the horse around and started away.

I stood in the morning sun, watching him go. Below me, the town I'd called home for the last few months was empty. I was confident I could find another horse and supplies to get me to my next destination. If I recalled correctly, the company Howard King worked for originated out of Denver City. That would be where I'd start my search for him. First, I'd get out of here and find a nice saloon to rest up in for a few days.

As I started down the mountain, my hat inexplicably blew back to me from wherever it'd been. I picked it up and reapplied it to my head.

The Red Duke

I follow Jim and Sonya toward the football stadium turned rock venue. Security checkpoints and fencing encompass every entrance. A whiff of pot drifts over from the parking lot. I savor the scent of the smoke and the electricity of the crowd.

Ahead of me, Sonya walks through the metal detector into Hazel Park Stadium. Jim follows her. I set my wallet and keys in the provided plastic bin, pass through the detector, and rejoin my friends while collecting my items.

Sonya motions toward the stage. "So, ready to see the Red Duke in person?"

"From a distance." Jim holds his ticket up to align with our section number in the nosebleeds.

"As long as we can hear him, who cares?" I head toward the concession stand.

As I walk, I'm surprised I don't need to weave my way through people. Most of the audience must still be pregaming in the parking lot. I grab my overpriced beers in record time and head to the merchandise table, where Jim and Sonya await me.

"We should check out the performance setup before we go to our seats." I hand out the drinks and take a big sip of my hoppy beverage.

"Nick, you're the expert. Lead on." Sonya bows low, pantomiming a serf's gesture to a king.

I throw my free arm out as if commanding an army. "Onward."

Jim chuckles at our shenanigans and follows us down the aisle between the folding chairs. The lower seating area covers the faded football lines. A girl walks past us in a shirt with the words "Howard King and the Crawling Chaos" emblazoned in bloody lettering.

Jim's head turns to follow her. "Why'd King change the act's name again?"

"It's an homage to David Bowie's Thin White Duke persona." As I finish, I realize how pretentious I sound.

Sonya smiles. "Like I said, you're the expert."

We enter the shadow of the enormous speaker stacks, and our approach is halted by barricades keeping us from getting within arm's reach of the raised performance space. The microphone stand, guitar, bass, keyboard, and drums stare at us from across the small gulf. The chest-high stage floor is covered in chalk-drawn occult symbols, with all the instruments encompassed in pentagrams connected to each other by straight lines.

"Reminds me of your necklace." Jim points to the collar of my plaid button-up.

I reach into my shirt and pull out the silver charm suspended by a leather cord. The talisman is a leaf shape, with five branches sprouting off a central limb, surrounded by an eye-like oval. I'd purchased it eight years ago for almost nothing at a dingy shop on Bleecker Street, during a folk music–inspired tour of Greenwich Village. "Carol almost broke up with me when I told her I was buying this."

Sonya nearly chokes on her beer. "That's rich. She's cheating on you with her coworker, and she threatens a breakup over your necklace choice?"

"Well, I didn't know she was cheating on me then. But now it's a totem to help me remember what a fool I was."

Sonya's expression changes to pity, and I feel my good vibes sliding away.

Jim shifts the subject back to the stage. "There's an ankh and the Eye of Horus."

"I see a few key shapes too," adds Sonya.

I point to one of the symbols nearest to us. It looks like a stick figure with a single angry eye. "That one is from the works of John Dee. He was an occultist who advised Queen Elizabeth the first. King became obsessed with it after recording his last record in England."

Jim chugs the rest of his beer. "So, what does the John Dee shape represent?"

I pull out my phone and take pictures of the stage. "Uh, the celestial elements, I think." I spin around and motion for Jim and Sonya to join me for a selfie.

We all smile as I stretch my arm out to capture us and the stage in frame. Once we're in position and smiling naturally, I take the picture. Jim and I start to turn back around.

Sonya doesn't move. "Hate it. I know I looked goofy. Let's do another."

Jim and I return to form as we snap a second group shot.

Sonya reviews the result. "Much better. We even got photobombed by someone."

They return to looking at the stage, leaning on the barricade for support. I zoom in on our picture. A guy stands in the shadows behind the drum kit, smiling maniacally. He's probably only a roadie, but the way the light catches his face makes his eyes look like inky pits. It causes me to shiver despite the summer heat. I check to see if I can spot the guy in person, but he's gone. When I post the image online, I edit him out.

Jim taps my shoulder. "Here come the fun police." He nods toward an approaching security guard.

"To the seats." Sonya mimics my commanding arm gesture from earlier.

We make our way back through the stadium and ascend the bleachers. My legs ache from climbing the aluminum stairs when Jim stops and points to our seats. Several settled attendees get up to let us pass to our designated spots on the bench. One portly fellow doesn't look happy as I squeeze past him and brush against his stomach. We make eye contact, and it becomes an awkward moment for both of us.

Jim reaches our assigned spaces and sits down, followed by Sonya. She sets her remaining beer on the ground between her legs. As my ass meets the firm metal, I immediately envy the people who brought plastic cushions.

Sonya pulls Jim and me into a hug. "So glad I get to be out with my two favorite guys."

Jim picks up Sonya's beer and polishes it off. "You see me every day."

"Yeah, but when we first started dating, Nick was with us all the time. We lived together for a year for god's sake. This feels like old times, and I love it."

"I had a ton of fun that year," I say, "but I'm glad I'm not sleeping on your floor anymore. The morning backaches from the air mattress were brutal."

Finished with the last of the alcohol, Jim is chattier. "Remember that night we listened to six hours of horror podcasts?"

"Yeah, we were all too scared to leave our apartment, even though we desperately needed toilet paper." I laugh at the memory.

Sonya stretches out her legs, and the light shimmers off her rainbow-colored boots. "As usual, it was left up to the woman to save the men."

"What about that time we came back to find Nick and Carol—" Jim abruptly cuts himself off. "Sorry. Didn't mean to bring her up again tonight. She's dead to us, dude."

"No worries. I'm over her." I certainly wasn't, but I didn't want to linger on the topic. "You can see the larger shape that all the stage symbols combine to form from up here."

Sonya plucks the plastic cup from my hand and claims the last gulp for herself. "Nick, you're the expert, what does it all mean?"

"I've seen some chatter online about the circles being," I pause to add air quotes, "magic stations." I look over the symbol formed by the interconnected chalk drawings. "And apparently each stop on the Red Duke's tour serves as another kind of station. One comment spammer was totally convinced that by moving from station to station the Red Duke planned to trigger mystical results."

A chilly gust of wind makes Sonya nestle into her boyfriend.

Jim clutches her tightly. "You think he'll play 'In the Mind of Madness'? I love that song."

I'm excited to play music aficionado again. "The last setlist I saw included it."

The sun dips behind the bleachers opposite us, and the first blast of bass booms out through the speakers. Everyone responds with a cheer as we stand to applaud the start of the show. The drummer crashes into the song as he hammers down on the cymbals before starting the backing beat. The stage remains dark until a spotlight flashes down on the guitarist, beginning the opening riff of "The Hermit in the Mirror." The bassist, drummer, and keyboardist are given their own lights; each band member is dressed in black from head to toe. They're all jamming at the center of their own chalk pentagrams. Huge screens flanking the stage come to life to broadcast a better view of the performance to the cheap seats. Only the Red Duke himself remains to be seen.

Vocals screech out to announce Howard King's arrival. "The Hermit climbs to the top of the mountain, but if you put him in the mirror, he shows you the monster."

I don't have any idea how the stage crew accomplishes it, but Howard King, the Red Duke himself, appears out of thin air on stage. My eyes alternate between the live band and the screens. King wears a crimson vest and dress pants of the same color. Unlike at past concerts, his wild locks are slicked back into a 1950s-style pompadour. As he raises his arms to the crowd, the sleeves of his white dress shirt fall and reveal freshly carved cuts matching the occult symbols on the stage.

Jim shouts over the song. "How much time do you think that paint took to apply?"

Sonya elbows him and shouts back. "Don't destroy the illusion."

I become consumed by the tune, and I'm grooving with everyone else as the band abruptly transitions into their next song, "Goat Headed God." As the music speeds up, I look over to see Sonya vanish. Before I can react, she's back and rocking out all the same, except the song is different now. We're on to "Baron's Tremble in the Lake of Langan," a slow melodic ballad.

Something hits my hand, and I shake it, thinking a bug has landed on me.

Amber liquid spills out over the crowd in front of me. Everyone glares back in anger as they try to dry off. I look down to see a half empty cup of beer in my hand. My mind struggles to make sense of this. I thought my drink had been empty, and I hadn't gotten a new one.

Sonya shakes her head. "Party foul."

I shout to my friends. "Where'd this come from? I didn't have this a second ago."

Jim leans over and takes the beer from me. "Calm down, man. Did you drink too much? I didn't think two beers would do you in."

"I never saw that thing glow before." Sonya points to my necklace.

I look down to see the leaf charm giving off a subtle blue hue.

The song ends, and King addresses the crowd. "You've been a great audience. We'll be back after a short break."

The color on the object hanging around my neck returns to normal. "What the fuck? What's going on. Did I miss the first set? Am I having a stroke? Are these stroke symptoms?" I sit down and take a deep breath.

Sonya sits next to me and rubs my back. "Calm down. Calm down. Jim, can you get him some water? Maybe he's having a bad reaction to something."

"Sure thing." Jim makes his way back down the aisle we'd come up.

People I'd spilled beer on venture off in search of something to dry themselves off with as they scowl at me.

"I didn't realize I had a beer in my hand," I say to the closest member of the departing group, a guy in designer sunglasses. "I'm sorry."

The guy shakes his head and follows Jim down the stairs. I notice the sun's gone now. Stadium lights illuminate the sky. Last I remembered, the sun was barely hidden behind the bleachers across from us. I can't catch my breath.

"Nick, relax. Did you smoke something we didn't see? Or take something?"

I shake my head in the negative.

"Well, maybe you just drank those beers too fast? Or maybe the heat's getting to you?"

As if in answer to her latest suggestion, an unseasonably cold gust makes us move closer together.

"Just take deep breaths. Squeeze my hand if you need to."

My fingers clutch hers tighter than I want to, and I try not to think about how she'd vanished a few moments ago. I need something else to focus on. "Describe the first set to me. What'd they play?"

"They opened with 'The Hermit in the Mirror,' jumped into 'Goat Headed God,' and I snuck down to get us some more beer while King introduced the band. When I came back, they were halfway through 'Pan's Delight.'" Sonya stopped to catch her thoughts. "Then there was 'Graveyard Dreamscapes,' 'What About Birds,' 'The Golem,' and 'Night Prince,' and they just wrapped up 'Baron's Tremble.'"

"I don't remember hearing anything between the start of 'Goat Headed God' and 'Baron's Tremble.'" My breathing starts to return to normal, and despite the bizarre situation, I can't identify anything physically wrong with myself.

"You just got too into the tunes," proposes Jim as he returns with a cup in his hand. "This will help. Nothing like a little water."

I chug down the refreshing liquid.

Sonya squeezes my hand. "So, you don't remember hearing 'What About Birds'? You loved that one!"

Taking a deep breath, I shake my head. Drums start echoing through the stadium as the second set begins. People are retaking their seats around us.

"Do you want to head out? We can just bail if you're not feeling good." Jim remains standing over me.

"No way. We all love the Red Duke's music. I can't make us leave. I'll just take it easy through this part of the show. I must've pushed myself too hard earlier."

Jim and Sonya look as if they are debating whether to listen to me, but then the guitar kicks in, and they turn toward the stage. My view is blocked by everyone getting to their feet to jam to "In the Mind of Madness." Jim turns to look at me, and we share an excited nod.

I continue taking deep breaths as the crowd goes wild. Sweat pours out of me, and I wonder if I'm dehydrated. I'd put in two twelve-hour days this week to make sure I'd caught up on work to be here. Light draws my gaze, and I look down to see my charm glowing again. The brightness increases while "In the Mind of Madness" reaches its crescendo.

I grab Sonya's arm to get her attention, and I'm disgusted to feel slime instead of skin.

King's lyrics reverberate through the air as the audience stomps along to the bassline. "You're all trapped in the mind of madness, and your freedom lies with me."

I look up.

Sonya's arm is covered in blood. Realization dawns on me. It's not blood on her arm; it's her exposed muscles. The skin is missing.

A hideous plop draws my gaze down to the aluminum bench.

Her lost skin is collecting in a doughy puddle next to me. I look back to Sonya. She's fixed on the show as her neck flesh starts to slide the same way as her arm's.

"Sonya?" I know I'm too quiet to hear over the raging guitar, but I'm terrified of what her reaction will be to what I'm seeing.

"One of you came with something special. You're in for the show of your life," King sings at the top of his lungs.

Despite the insanity of the moment, my brain recognizes that those aren't the usual lyrics to "In the Mind of Madness."

I look out at the crowd. Everyone else's skin is also sloughing off. I check myself and find that I'm the only one staying normal. The globs of flesh are oozing out and covering every trace of the bleachers. I lift my feet to avoid being touched by the spreading skin of the man whose stomach I'd grazed earlier. He looks at me and opens his mouth to say something when his face melts away.

I turn back toward Sonya to avoid the full horror of the man's new visage, but she's staring at me too. Her eyes roll back into her skull, and she collapses. Jim remains standing, focused on the show. He's not as far along in his deterioration as she is.

"No. No. Fuck no. Sonya." I dive forward to try to lift her up, but my hands sink into the liquifying remains of her body. "Jim, for god's sake. Help me. Your girlfriend is dying."

The keyboardist starts the intro to "Tremendum," and Jim's gaze never turns away from the stage. I think that might be a mercy as I withdraw my hands from Sonya. They're covered in a substance that feels like warm syrup mixed with Hamburger Helper. The white of Sonya's skull appears as the last of the flesh drips from her skeleton. I start to dry heave.

Jim chooses this moment to turn to me. "Why are they playing this song backward?"

I didn't notice it at first, but he's right. The keyboard solo is at the end of "Tremendum," not the beginning. As I stare at Jim, his body collapses in on itself. His head falls into his chest cavity, which crumples into his hips and causes his skeletal legs to topple.

I survey the stadium again, and I see nothing but bodily fluids and the crowd's remaining clothes. I retreat inwards. I'm fading from my own consciousness, and I peer out of my eyes like windows. I know I'm going to pass out soon, but I manage to stand.

The Red Duke's band continues to produce music from their pentagram-encircled stations on stage.

They all stare up at me.

As I peer back, their forms grow pale and thin. Writhing feelers replace their limbs as they jam onward. The Red Duke's head explodes in a burst of ichor as something slithers out of his body to replace it.

I rip my gaze away from the morphing performers, but I'm confronted by a new horror.

Among the folding chairs on the field, a black void is birthed from the fifty-yard line. Tendrils reach out to consume the nearest bits of flesh. Inside the darkness, something bright flares to life, and I see spheres circling a flaming beacon. I realize I'm looking at a solar system like it's outside my bedroom window. Space itself starts to blot out the star, and I see inky fingers smothering the sun. Then the light is extinguished as the malevolent expanse swallows the celestial body in its maw. A geyser of black fluid explodes out of the void, and three eyes, the color of burning coal, form in the sky.

As if released from paralysis, I take my first step toward escape, and I slip on a crowd member's lost skin and tumble down the bleachers. I land hard in a glob of flesh that used to be a person. Midnight comes for my mind.

2

A sharp pain brings me out of unconsciousness. I open my eyes. The sun glares down at me from a cloudless sky.

"You have to get out of here, or I'm going to call the cops." A security guard pokes me with his baton. "I'd really prefer to avoid the headache of getting the cops involved. So, why don't you just save me some paperwork and head home?"

My mouth is devoid of moisture, and my skin pulses with pain from where the sun's cooked me. "I—"

"Had too much to drink and wandered in here or got high and climbed the fence. I've heard it all before. So long as you're not hurt and nothing was damaged, you can leave without us making this a thing."

I struggle to my feet as the security guard watches. "My friends? The concert?"

"No concert this week. We've got a football game scheduled tomorrow. Now get going." The security guard points his baton toward the stadium exit.

Nothing remains of the show I'd watched. There's no liquified human remains, no chairs set up on the field, no living void spewing death out of a black hole. It's like nothing ever happened.

I check my pocket and am relieved to find my keys in place. I pull out my cellphone to find the screen cracked in several places. When I try to use it, I'm unable to get it to respond.

The security guard slams his baton against the aluminum bleacher, causing it to clang. "You're trying my patience." He holds his weapon toward the exit again. "Get out."

I start down the steps, and I continue looking for any signs of the Red Duke's concert. There's nothing. It's like it never happened.

When I reach the exit, the guard slams the gate loudly and locks it.

Before he can leave, I turn to face him. "What day is it? My phone's broke, I can't check."

The guard gives me a look of revulsion. "You need to clean your life up, kid. It's Saturday."

He walks away before I can ask another question. The concert was Friday, so Saturday means I was only out for the night if I didn't just imagine it all. Had I been on a drug bender? That would be like nothing I'd ever done before. I'd been afraid to try my roommate's low-grade acid in college.

I head toward my silver sedan, the only vehicle in the vast parking lot. Every step is worse than the last as I dry heave in my body's bid to expel any extra liquid to cool me down. My sweat is long gone. I must've been passed out beneath the sun for hours before the guard woke me.

When I reach the car, I open the door to vent the accumulated heat and immediately chug the warm bottle of water left in the center console. After sitting still with my eyes closed to recharge, I pull out my keys and start the vehicle. I crank the air conditioner to its top setting. As the air goes from hot to warm and finally to cold, the radio crackles to life.

"We've got the Red Duke himself in the studio today. He's dishing on his current tour, and we're dead excited to hear about his new song," the host announces. "So, what's this one called?"

"'The Sloughed Skin Show,'" the Red Duke says.

I picture my friends as liquified puddles of flesh on the stadium bleachers.

The host is ecstatic. "And what's it all about?"

"Oh, I never like to clearly state stuff like that. I like my listeners to make up their own minds, but I will say this one is inspired by the fans we've been enjoying on tour. Their sacrifices keep us producing."

I turn the radio off and put my foot on the gas.

3

When I barge into Jim and Sonya's apartment with the spare key they'd given me, nothing is out of place. Their orange cat, Lenny, charges forward and rubs against my legs. The couple is nowhere to be found.

"I'll be back," I say to the cat.

I leave the apartment and take the elevator to the lobby. The old woman at the front desk watches soap operas on an ancient portable television.

"Have you seen Sonya or Jim pass through here recently?" I ask.

She ignores me, and I knock the bell off her desk in anger. It clatters to the linoleum floor with a halfhearted jingle.

She looks up. "Can I help you?"

"Sonya and Jim? Have you seen them? Apartment 12-4!"

The receptionist goes back to her soaps. "No one lives in apartment 12-4. Please pick up the ringer on your way out."

"How do you explain the cat and all their stuff in there?"

The woman adjusts her glasses and stares up at me. "How would you know what's in there?"

I see her hand moving toward the panic button under the desk.

"Never mind. My mistake." I return the bell to the desk and head back to the elevator.

Fifteen minutes later, I slide the carrier containing Lenny into my backseat as a police car pulls into the parking lot. Part of me wants to run over and try to get the officers to listen to my story, but I know how it will sound. I'll end up committed.

4

When I get home to my apartment, I rush to the desk in my living room. I start my computer and locate hard evidence of Jim and Sonya's existence. All their social media pages are still up. Lenny's urgent meows break my attention from my monitor, and I open his carrier. He quickly meets my tabby cat, Helena. Neither feline seems happy with the other's presence.

I spend the next several hours trying to contact my lost friends, but I get no response. Their last posts are from before the concert. I reach out to Jim and Sonya's family members, but they all give me the same story. They've never heard of who I'm talking about. Even when I send direct links with pages clearly showing they're related; Jim and Sonya's parents deny knowing them.

Everything catches up to me at once, and I hit the floor and burst into tears. Sonya's melting body floods my mind as I try to visualize anything else. Jim's collapsing skeleton is there when I shut my eyes. The tide of blackness spewing out of the field swallows my consciousness.

I'm clutching my necklace tightly when my eyes open again. It's nearly midnight, and I'm sore from lying on the floor. I put out food and water for the cats before crawling into bed.

I'm back at the stadium. The keyboards in "Tremendum" play in reverse as Jim melts into goo next to Sonya. The inky patch opens before me, and the band mutates on stage. I look down at my neck, and I'm missing my glowing leaf charm. My stomach splits open, and my intestines fall onto the bleachers. I scream out as a slash appears in my forearm.

The bed is drenched in sweat, and my heart is pounding when I awaken, but I'm relieved to be at home instead of in the stadium. Helena is scratching at my wrist. I recoil in pain. She's clearly unhappy with the new visitor. My other hand confirms my necklace is still on. I get up for water and return to sleep, hoping not to dream again.

I wake to several missed calls from work, and I phone them with an excuse for not showing up. My track record is impeccable, so they don't argue with me. I vacate my bed, brew a cup of coffee, and get back on my computer.

I don't find much that helps, but I do find a few occult sites that list the leaf shape I'm wearing as a kind of protective ward. I try to recall the name of the store where I bought it, but I draw a blank. I even text Carol about it, and I'm surprised she gets back to me quickly and amicably, but she doesn't have the slightest idea about what the store's name was. Out of curiosity, I ask her if she remembers Jim and Sonya, but she only replies with question marks.

The enormity of the horror confronting me is too great. Faced with no good options, the lone act of retaliation I can muster is destroying my collection of Red Duke merchandise. I shove my deluxe vinyl albums, my CDs, and my t-shirts into a trash bag and proceed to smash everything with a hammer. The contents of the bag crunch and shatter under my blows. Once the bag is tossed into my apartment complex's dumpster, I focus on the only thing I can. I make Jim and Sonya's cat as comfortable as possible in his new home.

After He Wakes

1

"Pass the salt."

My sister responds without looking up from her phone.

I test her attention. "A black cat riding a unicorn just walked in."

Her finger scrolls up the screen, and she offers no acknowledgment.

I salt my canned peas and scoop them into my mouth. Chewing is a chore, but peas are all we've got. We'll need to make another scavenging run soon. Once I've swallowed, I shovel more into my maw. When there are only three peas left, I take one and fling it across the table.

"Mature, Matt." My sister wipes the smooshed pea off her forehead.

"Well, Laura, at least it got you off your phone."

"We live in an urban wasteland. The least you could allow me is a few minutes of freedom from our grim reality before my phone's battery dies."

I survey the room. Rubble from the collapsed second floor surrounds our unscathed table. A broken pipe from the upstairs bathroom drips into a stagnant puddle on the living room couch, and everything is coated in fine gray dust. My wheelbarrow is filled with some debris, but I've only just started to put this place right.

"Exploding Bubbles or Breaking Bricks today?"

"Neither. I was connecting dots."

"Oh. A new game? Let me play." I grab for the phone.

Laura holds the cell above her head. "Get lost, it's an old game, and it's my phone. Not my fault yours was crushed when he passed through."

I'm about to jump forward to snag the phone when the siren starts. We freeze in place. It blares long and loud like someone is blowing on the world's largest whistle. I feel like I'm going to go deaf if I don't shield my ears. The sound halts abruptly, but I can still hear it echoing in my head.

I grab Laura's wrist. "Basement!"

"But Mom and Dad?" She protests.

"We can either spend some time with corpses or become corpses ourselves."

The door bursts open. A shaggy-haired man in a gray hooded sweatshirt and jeans stares in at us. He points a gun in our direction before either of us can figure out what to make of him.

"Thought I heard voices in here. I've got a shelter. You'll be safe. Come on." Using his gun, he gestures for us to follow him and runs off.

Laura is at the doorway before I can stop her.

I remain seated. "Are you crazy? He's got a gun. We don't know him."

"You're right. He's got a gun. That's more than we have. Besides, I think I recognize him from somewhere in town. He's a local."

"What does it matter if he's from here? And what good is a gun against a gelatinous moving mountain? You watched the news the same as me. He made short work of our military, and we even got to watch him stomp our neighbors into jelly. Or maybe you forgot?"

She exits, and I'm left feeling guilty in the remains of our home. I can't leave the place I grew up. I can't leave Mom and Dad. But I can't leave my sister either.

Laura pops back into the doorway. "Come on. The gun won't stop him, but the weapon might stop his servants."

"Fine." I follow her.

Outside, storm clouds suffocate the sky. Rain starts pelting down on the ruined homes along East Middle Street. Laura gracefully dodges between wrecked cars while avoiding piles of shattered glass; she's been on the track team since eighth grade. At sixteen, she's got years of experience. I do my best to keep up, but I've spent my seventeen years playing video games. The armed stranger waits for us on the edge of South Stratton Street and beckons us to follow as he goes right.

There's a clamor of croaks off in the distance. His minions are almost here. The siren didn't give us much warning. Not that the early notice helped last time. I remember listening to a scientist on the news propose that he traveled within a storm to keep the environment wet for his followers. Another scientist thought the storm was just mother nature's natural reaction to something as unnatural as him. That was before our connections to the outside world were severed.

As we turn left on York Street, a flash of lightning illuminates the horizon to the right. His servants, dozens of creatures in human-like forms, are hopping and running into town, searching for food. It's only when they get close that you notice their fishy eyes, gills, and scaled skin. They travel before and after him, cleaning up his mess and eating those he doesn't pulverize into a paste. The top of his head appears in the distance, and I turn away.

Laura is staring at me. "Come on, you idiot. He's almost here." She breaks into a sprint toward our guide, who's a silhouette in the distance now.

I try and keep up as we zig and zag over fallen telephone poles and concrete blocks from shattered buildings. I nearly step on a downed wire before it spits sparks to let me know it's still live. After this, the way is a little clearer, and I run with all the energy I can muster until a side stitch threatens to send me sprawling. Just when I think I can't go any further, I find Laura stopped in the middle of Lincoln Square. I bend over, gasping for air. My lungs are on fire despite the cold rain.

"Where did he go?" I ask between gulps of oxygen.

"I don't know. I lost him. He went into one of these buildings." Laura scans the area frantically.

I look up to help her search. Most of the structures are still intact. The Farmers Market, the Pub, the David Wills Museum, the bank, and Union Pizza are relatively unscathed after his previous pass through the area. It's a minor miracle. The rain picks up speed, and puddles start forming at the edge of the road.

I get my breath back. "We have to go home. To the basement. We can't stay out here."

"Don't leave. You'll be my appetizer." One of his servants has outpaced the others, who are still far off down the street. This faux person is in a tattered trench coat, and he wears a wide-brimmed hat with water pouring off it. At a glance, you might mistake him for human. But only at a glance. His fishy eyes narrow, and he smiles wide, revealing a row of needle-like teeth. "Your people had their time on the surface. Now it's our epoch."

I push my sister behind me as adrenaline surges through my veins. He crouches down and prepares to leap at us. His legs bend like an amphibian's, despite his vaguely human stature. The gills on his neck pulse quicker, and I can literally see him getting excited by the prospect of eating us.

As he makes his leap, I freeze, unable to determine how to escape and save my sister.

A gunshot cuts through the rain, the thunder, and my fear.

Blood splashes me as the fish-frog's body smooshes into the pavement beside us.

Our guide, the man in the hooded sweatshirt, is holding his smoking gun in the entrance of Union Pizza. "Don't just stand around waiting for another Deep One. Get in here."

Laura pulls me along. I feel like I'm outside my body for a moment, watching us go into the pizza shop to stay alive a little longer when the world has already ended. She leads me past the seating and murals of Italy, behind the counter, into the kitchen, and down, through a metal hatch, into the basement. It's well-lit and spacious. Two cots are nestled into one corner. Metal shelves packed with canned goods line the walls, stacks of books, comics, and magazines fill the floor space, and a small doorway leads into a second, darkened room. I slowly return to a semblance of normality, or what passes for it these days.

"Deep One?" I ask.

The man in the hoodie walks to the darkened room and peers in before answering. "That's what they're called in *The Necronomicon*. We're supposed to have evolved from them, but I don't go for everything Alhazred has to say on the subject." He points to a particularly weathered book sitting atop one of the stacks in the room. "Not that introductions matter much anymore, but my name is Robert."

Laura chimes in. "I knew you looked familiar. You're the owner. I came in here to pick up pizza with my dad a few times. He said you guys went to high school together. I'm Laura, and this is Matt."

A memory crawls into my brain from the past. "Yeah, he said you had a comic signed by Alan Moore."

"Still do. It's in one of these piles."

Like that, I relax. The fact that this guy knew Dad takes the edge way off. I return to assess the sealed hatch. "Is this going to hold?"

Robert smiles. "Big green didn't get in here the last time he rolled through. The building is reinforced, and my father created this shelter to survive a Russian nuclear attack. We're as safe as can be. Not that he couldn't get in here if he wanted to. Our biggest advantage is that we don't rate as more than fleas to him."

I let out a sigh of relief and inspect the cans. There are peaches, corn, carrots, and, of course, more peas. On the bottom shelf, our savior has hundreds of military MREs stacked up. My grandfather had some of those. He let me try one once, not bad. Better than more peas. Exhausted from our travel through town, I let myself fall onto one of the cots, and I immediately feel bad for not asking permission.

Laura paces around the room and stops near the darkened doorway. "I was supposed to have a big track competition this month. Trained for ages. Guess you can't control when he decides to head your way though. Living with him is funny that way."

She goes to peek inside the other room, and Robert dashes toward her with the butt of his gun raised. "And now it's time for something that isn't too funny."

I get up and see my sister crumple to the ground with blood spilling from her head. I charge the pizza shop owner, and he spins the weapon around to meet my face. Everything goes black.

2

Pulsing pain in my cheek pulls me out of unconsciousness. I'm able to open both my eyes, but everything is blurry. A sharp stabbing in my tongue tells me at least one of my teeth is broken and jutting the wrong way. I try to speak and find my lips restricted by something sticky, duct tape.

My vision sharpens, and candlelight dances around the room. I look left and right to see ropes tied around my arms and legs. The restraints are secured to black pillars on either side of me. I can't relax my limbs, which are kept fully extended by my captor's handiwork. Robert stands in the center of the room, wearing only red boxer briefs. His girthy body is covered in red symbols. There are keys, stars, eagles, crosses, straight lines, and squiggly lines. His skin is now a collection of strange shapes. He continues to paint more on his right arm with a small brush in his left hand. At his feet, there is a bowie knife, duct tape, rope, and a circle drawn in chalk around his feet. Lines spread out from the ring and terminate in one of five tied-up people.

All of us are secured in the same way, with rope and duct tape. The way we're restrained forces our legs to form the outline of a five-pointed star. My sister is across from me, with blood trickling from her forehead. Her eyes are open in terror. Behind her, I see the doorway leading back into the supply-filled part of the shelter. An older man is to my right. He's vaguely familiar. A red-haired girl is to my left, her head wound is oozing pus, and I can smell the rot. Between her and my sister is a black-haired woman whose eyes are missing. Blood drips down from the empty sockets like tears.

Robert speaks. "Humanity's rule of earth ended the day Cthulhu rose out of the South Pacific Ocean. Our race had thought of itself as kings presiding over the planet, but we were only stewards for a greater being. Still, plenty of human empires have risen and fallen before. There's no reason to think Cthulhu will be the absolute end of life, and I may have found a way to halt his progress."

I struggle against my bonds, but the ropes around my wrists don't budge as I feel the rough fibers scraping away my skin. I'm not getting out of here. We're all this guy's captive audience. I study the other faces again, and I identify the man next to me. He's Mr. Campbell, my biology teacher from freshman year. The other girls are total strangers to me, and based on their conditions, I can't say I'm sorry not to be more familiar with them. That would only make this harder to bear.

Robert stops his painting and surveys us. "My grandfather opened Union Pizza in 1971. It's been a family-owned establishment ever since. A few fast-food corporations offered my father money for our location over the years, but he refused them all. That always made me proud. I was proud of my dad right up to the day he died." Our captor sets his brush down and gently blows on his freshly painted arm.

"Gettysburg is a smaller town than many realize. There are only about 8,000 people who reside within the area. Almost the entire economy is driven by war tourism. Middle-aged retirees and school children come from miles away to walk the fields where the Union defeated the Confederacy in the United States Civil War's climactic battle. Having grown up here, I learned to appreciate history, especially our state's history."

Robert smiles at his newest arm painting and moves to check the ropes on Mr. Campbell. He's careful not to disturb the chalk shapes he's drawn on the ground. He flicks the rope securing Mr. Campbell's left leg, and it barely shakes. Then Robert removes the man's left shoe and sock. My former biology teacher looks pissed, but he's as powerless as me. Robert returns to the center of the circle and grabs his bowie knife. The angry expression on Mr. Campbell curdles into fear. Robert slits the pad of my biology teacher's foot open. As blood pumps out, Robert replaces his bowie knife with his brush and dips it into the growing pool of crimson.

He begins tracing his chalk lines with the new pigment while resuming his monologue. "In fact, when I spent a summer in New York City pursuing my failed comic book dream, I never missed an opportunity to sing the praises of Pennsylvania. Philadelphia was the nation's original capital, and our state was one of the first to oppose slavery, thanks to our Quaker heritage. I also never missed an opportunity to remind residents that Manhattan was taken by the British in the Revolutionary War, and Staten Island was a British stronghold. Today, Staten Island is a Republican stronghold. So, I guess it stays red no matter the century."

Robert starts in on a new area of the floor with his brush. "Most people were surprised to find out that a good deal of both political parties were members of the Cult of Cthulhu, but I can't say that surprised me. It was interesting to note that the more polarized edges of the political spectrum were working together though. Never thought a Socialist and a Libertarian could agree on anything, much less their next god. You think you know people."

Robert pauses and makes a slit in the eyeless girl's foot, opening a fresh ink source for his bloody project. "Take me for instance. People look at me and see a pizza shop clerk. If they look a little closer and talk to me, they might realize I'm a creative pizza shop clerk who likes comic books. But nobody ever realized that the teens who've gone missing over the years ended up in my basement. I've been bleeding kids dry since I got back to town from New York. And here's the funny part, I was trying to bring Yog-Sothoth into our world. He's the gateway to infinite knowledge, and I wanted to know it all. I figured if I messed something up, at worst, I'd end the world in a blink. We'd be gone so quick we probably wouldn't notice. But then the stars became right for Cthulhu. Now we're all getting stomped on like ants instead of going out in a blaze of glory. Where's the dignity in that?"

I work my tongue against the tape on my mouth, trying to get it off. Each movement causes my broken tooth to shoot an ache into my brain. I worry I might knock myself out but being able to speak is my only tangible means of communication. If I can't convince him to let me and my sister go, at least I can tell him how crazy he is before I die. The ground shakes as the monster outside gets closer.

Our captor doesn't seem bothered as he continues working and talking. "You all know this, but the military tried confronting ole' big green when he first showed up. They started with tactical strikes, missiles, you name it. He just kept reforming. When governments sent in living soldiers, they went crazy and bled from their eyes. Most committed suicide, and some started attacking each other. The fools in charge launched nukes, but all that did was kill everyone but Cthulhu. Most of India was wiped out by us instead of the cosmic terror waltzing through the subcontinent. Haven't heard from the federal government since. They're probably held up in a bunker somewhere."

The maniac keeping us hostage laughs to himself as he gently strokes his bloody brush back and forth on the floor. "Still, life goes on. Most of the world has started to adjust to living with Cthulhu. It's not that much different from avoiding a hurricane. Major cities in his path are evacuated, those that can't leave batten down the hatches, and when he's passed by, we all come out of our hidey-holes. Us humans are a lot like cockroaches now. Except Cthulhu is the light that sends us scurrying for the corners. Man, I miss Dad."

Robert moves toward my sister, and my heart beats faster. I resume my effort to escape the ropes around my wrists, but my skin is rubbed raw to no avail. I'd give anything to die without having to watch this psycho hurt my sibling.

"He's the one who first shared *The Necronomicon* with me. A copy has been passed down in my family for generations going all the way back to the Alhazred, or at least that's what Dad would have you believe. In truth, my research points to our copy originating in Arkham. The witch trials there were short but bloody. The judge who sentenced eighteen witches to death by drowning was my dear old ancestor, and I have always theorized that the reason he chose to drown those witches was because he struck some kind of bargain with the Deep Ones who used to swim in and out of the Miskatonic River. But that's just my pet theory."

Robert moves past Laura, and my heart's beating slows a little.

"What is a fact is that my ancestor recorded being given the book by a black-robed man at a crossroads at midnight. Of course, that must've been Nyarlathotep himself. Don't believe me? Well, there's a sketch of him in the judge's journal that makes it pretty much indisputable. Seeing is believing as they say. Of course, I only had access to that journal for a little while when I visited the Arkham Museum of History, but, well, just take my word for it, and my word is as good as an Innsmouther's gold."

The red-haired girl gets her lips around her tape. "What do you want with us? Just let us go. Please. That monster outside will kill us all anyway."

Robert picks up the duct tape and applies a fresh piece to cover her mouth. I'm surprised she had the energy for the plea with her head leaking pus. I keep working on my own tape despite the obvious futility.

Once the girl is silenced, Union Pizza's resident occultist resumes his long tale. "Well, I was getting to that. You see, I could roll over like a dog and adjust to life with Cthulhu, sure. But, well, Gettysburg is where the Confederacy died. I'm proud of that. Just a few miles west is Shanksville. That's where those brave Americans fought off the terrorists who'd hijacked their plane on 9-11. They didn't survive, but they heroically saved countless lives by stopping those villains. And that was here in Pennsylvania too. So, you see, two great threats to these United States were thwarted in the Keystone State. I think it's as good a place as any to end Cthulhu."

Robert drops the tape and picks the knife back up. "I've read and reread *The Necronomicon*, *The Midnight Path*, *The King in Yellow*, and I think I found just the spell to do it. We don't need to kill him; we just need to give him the monster's equivalent of a lullaby. Once he's asleep again, I can go back to trying to summon Yog-Sothoth, and, at worst, end the world in a kinder, gentler way.

Of course, if everything goes as planned, you won't be here to see any of this. Your blood is a major component of the ritual. I'll need buckets of it to draw the needed symbology. Please don't take this personally. Your sacrifice probably won't be in vain. And if it is, I'll gain valuable experience on how to perfect the spell."

The maniac walks back over to the red-haired girl, and he imbeds the knife in her throat. It goes in like a fork through cake. Blood bubbles up and oozes out of the wound. Air is sucked into the puncture as the blade comes out, and she chokes and struggles as she dies. Then he's onto Mr. Campbell. The man who taught me biology is dead before the knife's removed from his carotid artery. Robert's careful not to let any squirt out to ruin his work on the floor before he moves over to the eyeless woman and finishes her off with a slice. He moves toward my sister.

I bite down hard and get the tape off my mouth. "Hey, psycho. If you're going to end us all, at least end me first."

Robert stops his approach toward Laura. He picks up the duct tape and moves in my direction. As he unrolls a large piece, the earth starts to rumble.

I smile. "Sounds like big green is near."

In a blink, the roof is gone, and we're all being pelted by rain. The intricate pattern Robert drew on the floor is washed away. A lightning flash reveals my savior. Cthulhu looms above us as big as a mountainside. He reeks of what I imagine a thousand open graves might smell like. Globs of greenish ichor drip from his skin, generating a steaming hiss where they land. His face of tentacles draws closer to us, and I realize he's bending forward. His eyes glow like burning coal. The remains of Union Pizza's structure are clutched in his talons.

I laugh like a lunatic. "You did it. Your spell managed to get his notice. You're the cockroach who drew Cthulhu's attention."

Robert looks at me, and I see panic flood his face for the first time. "Yog-Sothoth, hear my plea."

He raises his knife, and I see the point with more focus than anything else in the whole world. Robert's still going to try to kill me. There's some insanely stubborn part of his brain that thinks he can finish the ritual.

One of Cthulhu's facial tentacles slithers down around Robert. He's gone in the next instant. I watch him rise into the sky, and blood rains back down. His legs follow a moment later. Then his upper half lands in the middle of his ruined circle. His eyes stare at me.

"I was touched by a god," Robert says before his face goes lifeless.

Deep Ones swarm into the ruined shelter. Two of them open their fishy maws to consume our captor's legs, meeting in the middle. Three others split his upper half. Arms, head, and midsection are taken by different monsters who hop away happily. More fish-frogs spill into the remains of the room. They swarm to the corpses of the others. I look over at my sister. We lock eyes with each other as we await our turns to be food.

Above us, Cthulhu turns away, and the earth shakes. Rubble from the resulting destruction piles into our hole. I lose sight of my sister and the world.

3

Laura is the first thing I see when my eyes glimpse light again. I'm sure I'm dead until the pain starts. My wrists burn from struggling against the ropes, and my side is in agony from where one of the pillars pinned me down. But I'm alive and so is Laura. Three men work frantically to help me out of the rubble.

She points up. "Look."

The sun is shining down on us for the first time in weeks. Cthulhu must've left the area. There are other people here too. Residents who managed to weather the storm are streaming down into the rubble pit to help my sister and me. We're cockroaches swarming out of our holes now that it's safe. That's all we'll ever be while Cthulhu is awake.

If you're reading this, it means I've failed to stop this book's publication, but I managed to sneak this warning into the file sent to the printers.

My name is Elijah Dayne Morock, and I've known Jeremiah for as long as I can remember. When we were in elementary school together, an art teacher was forced to tape Jeremiah's mouth shut to keep him from bewitching her. Don't believe me? Check out Jeremiah's YouTube channel.

As a teenager, Jeremiah visited the lost town of Centralia, the cursed Weatherly Cemetery, the spot of the Shepton Mine Disaster, and, of course, the sights where the Lattimer and Sugarloaf Massacres occurred. He absorbed the tragic histories around his hometown of Hazleton, Pennsylvania, and now he's using them to fuel his fictional town of Hazel Peak.

In his twenties, Jeremiah broadened his aggregation of dark energy. He visited the graves of disturbed individuals such as H.P. Lovecraft and Edgar Allan Poe. He communed with lost souls like Shirley Jackson, Robert W. Chambers, and Robert E. Howard. He spent four years in the bowels of New York City, searching for hidden secrets. This was all done in the service of creating A Mythos of Monsters and Madness.

How do I know all this? Until recently, I was Jeremiah's best friend. You see, Jeremiah created this anthology to entrap the minds of his readers. He used the occult lessons he learned throughout his life and wove them into his narratives. I know this sounds like lunacy, but Jeremiah confessed it all to me. He thought

I'd serve as his right hand in the world he intends to spawn. When I voiced reservations, he threatened to banish me from existence. I'm praying that he was bluffing but based on the magical demonstrations he's given me over the years, I confess that I believe he has the power to do what he threatens. Those who manage to finish all his tales will be marked by beings beyond their understanding. Consuming this collection serves as a key that unlocks the gate to those who dwell outside our reality. If you've read through all his stories, the Living Void now has your scent, he isn't just Jeremiah's fictional creation.

For your sake, I hope you found my warning before you finished each section of this book. If not, I can only offer you my sympathy.

Story Notes

Feeding Time

While attending Seton Hill University, I was working on a fantasy novel for my thesis, and I kept finding myself wanting to take a break from that to write short horror stories. An ad for the Ligonier Valley Writers 2018 Flash Fiction Contest was left on the table in the break room of Seton Hill during my Summer Residency there, and I decided to enter the contest. To my shock, Feeding Time took first place. I used the resulting prize money to pay my apartment's water bill to satisfy a requirement Stephen King put forth for being a writer in On Writing: A Memoir of the Craft, that being that you use your writing income to pay a bill.

The Hungry Cemetery

This story began on my first wedding anniversary. Due to COVID-19, my wife and I couldn't go on our honeymoon to the United Kingdom. Instead, we kept things simple and started our day with a hike near Carlisle, Pennsylvania. We encountered a strikingly odd, decrepit cemetery just off the trail, and I immediately started pitching the story of The Hungry Cemetery to my wife. Six months later, Benjamin T. Lambright reached out to me and asked if I'd be interested in submitting to Purple Wall Stories. I submitted The Hungry Cemetery to their monthly writing competition, and I was delighted to see it win story of the month for February 2021. It was subsequently printed in their Big Purple Book of Badass Stories: 2022.

Lost Vintage

My first draft of The Hungry Cemetery took a strange turn when a blue-haired ghost woman appeared in my graveyard. I decided to go with the weird twist, and I shifted my story to try to see if I could make it jive with a Gothic submission call I'd recently seen for Castle of Horror Anthology Volume 4: Women Running from Houses. Thankfully, the resulting story came out pretty good, and the anthology editor, Jason Henderson, accepted my offering. This story was also adapted into a fantastic audio version by Bridgette Brenmark on The Weird Library. Go give it a listen.

Legend Trip

This previously unpublished piece was written for a NoSleep Podcast flash fiction submission call. It started as an original piece, but like the story it's connected to, this one had a mind of its own. It ended up becoming a prequel to Lost Vintage.

The House Flipping Find

I started to listen to the NoSleep Podcast daily somewhere around 2016. I'd been a fan of Creepy Pasta stories, such as that of Slender Man, since college, and I was overjoyed to find a podcast dedicated to those types of tales. I saw the podcast live twice, and I'd submitted a few stories that weren't accepted before The House Flipping Find made it onto the program. This is, to date, my proudest writing accomplishment. Getting to be a tiny part of the amazing NoSleep Podcast is an outstanding honor. Many thanks to Olivia White and the whole crew there for creating such a fabulous audio adaptation of my work. Lastly, I must give kudos to Mr. Bobb for a helpful tweak to the text.

Monster in the Mine

This was the last story selected for inclusion in this collection. It was published in 2024 but written in 2020, in response to a call for stories by the Horror Writers Association. The story was rejected for that anthology, Other Fears, but I liked the tale, so I kept submitting it, and it eventually found a home. The car accident featured is based on a real-life incident that happened to me when I was learning to drive in high school. My vehicle's break line snapped going up a snowy hill, and I narrowly avoided flying off the road, and the mountain I lived on, by jerking the wheel so I hit a snowbank on the side of the road, while falling backward. The historical events relayed by Carolyn, who also pops up in "The House Flipping Find," are based on true occurrences from my hometown. Lastly, I didn't realize it when I wrote it, but on rereading it, I see this story as a kind of subversion of Stephen King's *It*.

The Abyss Within

After "The House Flipping Find" was adapted by NoSleep, I immediately started to worry I would be a one hit wonder on the podcast. Thankfully, this story proved me wrong. I wrote this while I was contemplating my coming fatherhood. It's one of a few tales I wrote during my wife's pregnancy that dealt with kids. Once again, I must thank the entire NoSleep Podcast crew for turning my story into a fantastic audio program.

Seven Entries in the Midnight Path

I wrote this story after being inspired by "Notes for the Barn in the Wild" from Paul Tremblay's collection, *Growing Things*. Of course, H.P. Lovecraft's *The Necronomicon* and *The King in Yellow* are both inspirations as well, both being works that drive their readers insane. It took a while to get published, but I used that time to refine and edit it. One thing I added was Dr. Kiste, who is named in honor of the outstanding horror writer Gwendolyn Kiste.

Our King Needs Subjects

I originally wrote this as an audio script for the NoSleep Podcast, but when it was rejected, I liked the story's concept so much that I changed it into a prose tale. POGs were big when I was a kid, and I remember having a solid collection. There's also a piece of artwork with the King in Yellow holding up the Yellow Sign on a small circular disk that reminded me of a POG.

The Threshold

I'd had a version of this story kicking around my head going back to 2013, and I decided it was time to purge it from my system. I wrote this in monthly installments for New Pulp Tales. The excellent writer, E.C. Skowronski, provided edits for the entirety. Interestingly, the video game *Control* introduces a similar concept as the one I used in my story with thresholds to other realities appearing at random. We probably arrived at the concept independently, but it's odd when stuff like that happens. For the record, my story came out first. Although, we both owe a dept to Stephen King's *The Drawing of the Three*, where I first encountered the free-standing doorway to another dimension idea.

The Sheriff and the Samurai

This story came into existence because I showed some friends, Tom and Joey, the movie *Bunraku*. The movie isn't critically well regarded, but I think it's a pulpy, campy classic. The movie focuses on a cowboy without a gun and a samurai without a sword teaming up to take out a villain in a dystopian future. I decided to do my own version, but I set my story in the 1800s, gave my heroes their classic weapons, and I introduced

Weird Fiction elements. The talented writer, Lucas Click, provided edits for this tale when it appeared on New Pulp Tales.

The Red Duke

I love David Bowie, and I especially love his song and album Station to Station, which he put out while he was in his Thin White Duke persona. For those who don't know, Bowie was into ritual magic and Station to Station has to do with that subject. I also crammed this story with references to works and names from some of my favorite horror writers such as John Langan, Laird Barron, and Paul Tremblay. While revisiting this tale, I realized it owes a major debt to John Langan's "Outside the House, Watching for the Crows."

After He Wakes

I wrote this for a Lovecraftian Fiction call for Flame Tree Press. The story didn't make the cut, but I was elated when Mike Davis published it on the Lovecraft eZine's Patreon page. If you like Lovecraftian horror, you should be listening to and supporting the Lovecraft eZine. They all do great work for the horror community. The story was also subsequently re-published in Lost Tales: Beyond Monstrosity from the wonderful Cabbit Crossing Press.

Acknowledgements

I must first thank my mother and father. My mother inspired the love I have for horror, fantasy, and all things cool. My father gave me the work ethic I needed to be a writer. Then there is my wife, who as the dedication says, is my first reader for everything. In addition to that, she supports me in countless ways. I can't thank her enough for being my wife. Of course, I must also thank my daughter, who inspires me beyond words. In addition to those members of my family, I'm thankful for everyone in my clan, grandparents, aunts, uncle, brothers, cousins, mother-in-law, extended family, who have supported me in my crazy pursuit of being a published author over the years.

Next to thank are my many supportive friends. Don (my first collaborator), James, Oliver, Caso, Dave, Adam, DeRosa, Steve, Laura, Shay, Chelsea, Jeff, and Cass have all cheered me on over the years. Trish is a high school friend who never failed to believe I could make it as a writer, even when I was doubting myself. A special thanks to Phil, for the use of his eldritch library, and Tom, for conspiratorial discussions. Thanks as well to my New Pulp Tales gang, the League of Extraordinarily Odd Gentlemen, my friends in the Horror Writers Association, my co-workers (especially Maggie who encouraged me to pursue tuition reimbursement for graduate school), my Seton Hill classmates and teachers, and the Lovecraft eZine crew. Those groups are all filled with extremely supportive pals. If you're a friend who has ever listened to me talk writing, encouraged me, or read my work, I thank you too. I have a special thanks to give to Jason Henderson for publishing several of my tales and giving me a blurb for the front cover. I must also thank John Langan for offering so much of his time to listen to me in person and indulging my various fan celebrations of his work online.

Next there is my high school creative writing teacher, Mrs. Bromiley, who gave me the confidence to believe I might be able to be a real author one day. There are many other teachers, professors, and writers who offered encouragement and support to me along the way. I thank them all for their help in getting to this point. Jason Jack Miller, Heidi Ruby Miller, Rachel Hollander, Robert Delfino, Fr. Bob Pagliari, and Paul Goat Allen all deserve extra acknowledgement. I'd go on listing people, but my fingers would fall off before I finished.

Lastly, I want to thank you for reading this work. I hope you enjoyed it. If you didn't, I hope it at least distracted you from something worse for a little while.

Publication Credits

"Feeding Time": Ligonier Valley Writers 2018 Flash Fiction Contest, 2018.

"The Hungry Cemetery": The Big Purple Book of Badass Stories: 2022, Benjamin T Lambright, 2021.

"Lost Vintage": Castle of Horror Anthology Volume 4: Women Running from Houses, Jason Henderson and In Churl Yo, 2020.

"Legend Trip": Original to this Collection.

"The House Flipping Find": NoSleep Podcast Episode 8, Season 14, 2020.

"Monster in the Mine": Castle of Horror Anthology Volume 11: Revenge, Jason Henderson and In Churl Yo, 2024. Originally published as "The Monster in the Mine."

"The Abyss Within": NoSleep Podcast Episode 4, Season 18, 2022.

"Seven Entries in the Midnight Path": Castle of Horror Anthology Volume 7: Love Gone Wrong, Jason Henderson and In Churl Yo, 2022.

"The King Needs Subjects": Original to this Collection

"The Threshold": New Pulp Tales, E.C. Skowronski, 2021.

"The Sheriff and the Samurai": New Pulp Tales, Lucas Click, 2021.

"The Red Duke": Vinyl Cuts, Cin Ferguson, 2024.

"After He Wakes": The Lovecraft eZine Patreon Page, Mike Davis, 2021.

About the Author

Jeremiah Dylan Cook is a writer who wants to give you nightmares that delight and excite. His work has been published by The NoSleep Podcast, Castle Bridge Media, Tales to Terrify, Ghost Orchid Press, Scary Dairy Press, Cabbit Crossing Publishing, Timber Ghost Press, The Lovecraft eZine, The Weird Library, Hippocampus Press, and others. He's won two writing contests and received the Mario Mezzacappa Memorial Award for Outstanding Achievement in Poetry and Prose while pursuing his bachelor's degree at St. John's University. Jeremiah completed his Master of Fine Arts in Writing Popular Fiction at Seton Hill University and is the managing editor of New Pulp Tales.com. You can learn more about his diabolical deeds and eldritch emanations at www.JeremiahDylanCook.com.

www.ingramcontent.com/pod-product-compliance
Lightning Source LLC
Chambersburg PA
CBHW022044240626
47154CB00007B/2558